# ON THE COME UP

Also by Travis Hunter

*At the Crossroads*

*Two the Hard Way*

Published by Kensington Publishing Corp.

# ON THE COME UP

## Travis Hunter

Dafina KTeen Books
KENSINGTON PUBLISHING CORP.
www.kensingtonbooks.com/KTeen

DAFINA KTEEN BOOKS are published by

Kensington Publishing Corp.
119 West 40th Street
New York, NY 10018

All Kensington titles, imprints, and distributed lines are available at special quantity discounts for bulk purchases for sales promotion, premiums, fund-raising, educational, or institutional use.

Special book excerpts or customized printings can also be created to fit specific needs. For details, write or phone the office of the Kensington Special Sales Manager: Attn. Special Sales Department. Kensington Publishing Corp., 119 West 40th Street, New York, NY 10018. Phone: 1-800-221-2647.

K logo Reg. US Pat. & TM Off.
Sunburst logo Reg. US Pat. & TM Off.

ISBN-13: 978-0-7582-4252-5
ISBN-10: 0-7582-4252-2

First Printing: November 2011
10 9 8 7 6 5 4 3 2 1

Printed in the United States of America

*This novel is dedicated to the Hearts of Men Foundation.*

# Acknowledgments

It amazes me that I'm writing "thank-yous" for my tenth novel. I never thought I'd get past number one; and if it wasn't for you all, I wouldn't have. I thank you all from the bottom of my heart. I hope you'll enjoy *On the Come Up* as much as I enjoyed writing it.

I would like to thank God for all of His blessings, and my son, Rashaad Hunter, for being the best kid in the entire world. Linda Hunter, for you are the best mother a guy could ask for. Dr. Carolyn Rogers, for always encouraging me to reach for the stars. Carrie Moses, Sharon, Christina, Aaron and Moses Capers, Andrea and David, Trevor and Tyler Gilmore, BRITTANY GILMORE☺, Lynette, James (Ray Ray), Barry Moses. Amado and Amari, Hunter and Ruth Rogers, Ron Gregg, Gervane Hunter, Ahmed, Ayinde, Shani, Jibade, Taylor and Sherry Johnson, my uncle Clifton Johnson, Mary and Willard Jones, Pam and Rufus, Monica (Imani) McCullough, Janera Jones, Nazarrah Rivera, Trina Broussard, Rolanda Wright, Katrina Leonce and all the Sisters Sippin' Tea, and all of the wonderful book clubs who read my novels. Willie and Schnell Martin, Lakecia Griffin, my agent Sara Camilli, my editor Selena James, Mercedes Fernandez, Zane, and Melody Guy for getting this started and for setting the editorial bar very high from the start.

To all of the wonderful people who help run the Hearts of Men Foundation: Tammy Martin, Tonietta Wheatle,

Richard Stewart, Alisa Jones, Lester Rivers III, Stefon Shilo, Jeff Cleveland, Terry Boyd, LaMont and Brandon McIntosh, Maurice Kelly, and all of the kids who keep us busy.

My industry folks: Jihad, Eric Jerome Dickey, Victoria C. Murray, Lolita Files, R.M. Johnson, Kendra Norma Bellamy, Carol Mackey, Chandra Sparks Taylor, Brian Eggeston, Nzingah, Oniwosan, Pearl Cleage, Tee Cee Royal, Tricia Thomas, Ruth Gadson, Kim and Will Roby, and Kannik Sky.

If I neglected to mention your name, charge it to my head not my heart.

# 1

## DeMarco

"**R**esident DeMarco Winslow," said a loud voice over the intercom. "Please report to your room."

I listened in closer. "Did they just call my name?" I said to Coo Coo, one of my friends from the neighborhood where I grew up.

"I think so, homie," he said. "Whatchu do?"

"I haven't done anything," I said with a frown as I thought back to what I may have done. I stood from my desk and closed my textbook. "I wonder what they want."

"You better go see," Coo Coo said. "Maybe you going home, boy?"

"That would be nice," I said. "But I doubt that."

"No other reason for them to be calling you."

I thought about what my friend said for a second and realized that he was right.

"Hold it down out there until I get home," Coo Coo said with a blank expression on his brown baby face. He reached out to shake my hand as if he was congratulating me, but we both knew going home wasn't anything to celebrate.

Coo Coo was in for stealing a candy bar from a gas station, and the owner of the store was acting like he was a bank robber. He pressed charges and the judge gave my friend nine months in the pokey for a doggone Snickers bar. He was only fourteen years old and already seemed to be getting the hang of life behind the fence. Coo Coo had lived a very hard life and his eyes told his story: sad, droopy, and void of any signs of a future. His mother was in prison and his father was shot and killed during a botched bank robbery. Coo Coo lived with an aunt who treated him like he was a leech. He got his nickname because folks always called him crazy, but he was as sane as anyone else. He only acted crazy to keep the nuts away.

"Resident DeMarco Winslow. Please report to your room," the voice said again.

I sighed and picked up my drawing tablet and walked to the front of the class. Officer Scales appeared in the doorway and nodded at me. That was my cue that he would be escorting me back to my "room." I don't know why they called them rooms; I guess it was because we were juveniles and they wanted to be politically correct, but in my book, they were cells and we weren't residents, we were inmates.

Officer Scales asked, "How ya doing, boy?" He was at least six feet ten inches tall and was mostly muscle.

"I'm good."

I followed him out of the classroom without a word to any of the thirty or so other kids who looked and dressed

just like me. We were a sea of black faces, navy-blue jump-
suits, and orange flip-flops.

"What's going on, Scales?" I asked as we walked side by
side. "Why they want me?"

"Don't know, lil buddy," Scales said. "Maybe you have a
visitor. Today is your birthday, right?"

"What's the date?"

"August twentieth," he said.

"Oh yeah? Well, I guess it is," I said with a hunch of my
shoulders.

"Yeah," Scales said. "The staff here was trying to do a lil
something for you this morning, but the new director is a
butt-wipe and he shut it down."

"It's all good. Don't nobody wanna celebrate their
birthday up in here anyway," I said as if I had a better place
to be.

Scales chuckled, then used his large key to open the
steel door leading to the main building. We entered
through the cafeteria, walked through the commons area,
past the control booth, then down a hallway all the way to
my "room."

"Happy birthday, DeMarco," a short, white nurse said as
she walked by.

"Thanks," I said, thinking of how many birthdays I had
spent in this place.

"How old are you now, Dee?" Scales asked.

"I'm sixteen, man. Getting old."

Scales stopped in front of my "room" and opened the
door.

"I've been working here for four years and for four
years you've been coming in and out of this place. When

are you going to wise up and realize that you are better than this, Dee? You're a good guy, man. I mean you could really be somebody, but you gonna have to leave that street crap alone or whatever it is that keeps bringing you back here. I know I wouldn't want to keep coming back to jail all the time. People like you, and you're smart. Those are two of the best qualities anyone could ask for, and you just take it for granted and throw it away by coming in here."

I nodded my head but didn't say anything. What was there to say to that? Once he had my door open, I walked in. I looked at my bed and there was an empty box sitting on my bunk. That could only mean one thing—I was leaving.

Scales held out his hand and I shook it.

"I don't wanna see you come in here no more, boy. Take my number down. If you're hungry or something, call me. Just stop doing the stupid stuff, man. When you turn seventeen it's over to the big jail, and that's when it gets real," he said, slapping his huge paw on my shoulder.

I nodded my head, but I wasn't really paying him any attention. It was always so easy for folks to sit back and judge me. They didn't have a clue as to what I had to deal with when I went home, and truth be told, I wasn't really looking forward to going there.

"Don't just stand there looking crazy, go find something to write my number down on," he said.

I walked over to the metal desk that was bolted to the concrete wall and wrote down his number on a piece of paper.

Once Scales had stepped away from my room, I gathered my personal items: my drawing tablets, a shoe box containing my tattoo supplies, and a brush for my waves. I walked out into the hallway and waited to be escorted to the intake building where I would be sent on my way. As I stood there waiting, I saw Prodigy Banks. We called him Mr. P. He was a volunteer teacher who was also a mentor to a lot of the real knuckleheads at the facility.

Mr. P was about six-feet-three-inches tall, had a bald chocolate head, and everyone seemed to love him. Especially the female employees. They just blushed and blushed whenever he walked by, but from my viewpoint he never paid them any mind. There was something about Mr. P that said he was above all of the drama. He was very passionate about helping his boys, as he called us. We hit it off one day after I had gotten into a fight and was sent back to my room for "cool down," which was exactly what it sounded like. Mr. P came by my room, had one of the officers open my door, and handed me a book. He told me that I needed a little something to kill the boredom of being forced to sit in a six-by-six space for the next twenty-four hours. Before that day, I had never read a book on my own. He was smart enough to give me something I could relate to. It was a book by a self-published author called Bliz. The book was interesting and it made me want to read more. Before long I went from street fiction to reading Sun Tzu's *The Art of War*.

Mr. P motioned for me to come his way and I walked over to where he was standing. The intake building was directly behind him so I strained my eyes to see if I could catch a glimpse of my mother, but the lobby seemed empty.

"You ready?" he asked.

"Yeah," I said, confused as to why he was asking me that question. "Who signed me out?"

"I did," he said. "Go on and give these folks their clothes back. I'll be waiting right here."

He didn't have to tell me twice. I was authorized to be released three weeks ago, but my sorry mother never came to sign me out, so I was stuck here until I could find a relative or somebody who the officials at Metro trusted enough to vouch for me. Sitting in jail after your release date was all a part of being a poor black boy from the hood. If I had to sit and calculate how much extra time I had done after my release dates, I might be close to a year. Thanks, Mom.

I quickly changed clothes and jumped back into the same ones that I came in with over six months ago. The jeans were a little too snug around the waist and somehow they seemed to have shrunk to where the pant legs ended at my ankles. I forced my size twelve feet into the size eleven Air Max 95s. My feet were killing me already, my pants were too short, and my shirt was too tight. I looked a hot mess, but that too was part of the drill. I balled up that blue jumpsuit and threw it in the empty laundry cart. The flip-flops that I wore were cheap and were already falling apart, but I placed them on the shelf for some other poor soul to wear. Five minutes later, I was on the other side of the steel doors that kept me trapped for so long.

I said my good-byes to the intake staff, just like I had done so many times before, and then stepped outside into the Georgia heat.

*Good Lord,* I thought as the humidity attacked my nostrils.

It was hot and humid, but there was something about being on the other side of that fence that made it a little cooler. I looked up at the thirty-feet-high gates that were topped off with razor wire and exhaled. I didn't hate this place; actually, I had been here so many times that it had almost become a second home.

"Are you gonna stand there staring at this place all day, or do you wanna leave?" Mr. P asked with his hands outstretched.

"I'm coming," I said, shaking my head as I continued to stare back at the place that housed some of Atlanta's worst kids. "Thirty-two."

"Thirty-two?" Mr. P asked.

"I've been here thirty-two times," I said, not believing the number myself. "Thirty-two times. That's crazy."

"Well, don't make it thirty-three. Let's go," Mr. P said. "It's hot out here."

I looked away from the kiddy jail that raised me and up to the sky. I gave God a wink and turned away. I walked with Mr. P down the long walkway to the parking lot as I thought about some of the past mistakes I made that had landed me in the pokey.

I'm not a bad kid. As a matter of fact, I'm a pretty good one. Every single time that I've been arrested, it wasn't because I got caught doing something stupid, it was calculated. When I was twelve years old, a friend from my neighborhood came home bragging about how well he was fed and how the juvenile center had all of these video games, a pool table, basketball courts, and a big-screen television. To a lot of kids, having those things was the norm, but to me they were luxuries I'd only seen on television. To me, going to juvenile hall was an opportunity to never be hungry. Three hot meals every day was like dying and going to heaven. So whenever I got hungry or cold or just plain tired of living where I was living, I would go steal something from a store and make sure I got caught.

"So," Mr. P asked me. "What was all that staring about?"

"I just wanna make sure this is the last time I ever see it," I said.

He nodded his head but didn't say anything.

"There was a time when I didn't mind coming here, but it's time to move on to bigger and better things."

"I hear ya, but you have to do more than talk, my tattoo-faced friend. Choices, Dee. Life is all about choices. But," Mr. P said, hunching his shoulders, "you should've never been here in the first place."

"You keep saying that, Mr. P, but I'm guilty as sin," I said as I walked beside him on the walkway.

"Yeah, but not really," Mr. P said. "You're what I would call a victim of circumstance. Doesn't excuse what you did, but . . . whatever. That's the past. I don't like to spend too much time dwelling there."

I stared at the man. He was by far the coolest dude I'd ever met, but I didn't trust him outside of those walls. What was his angle?

"Thanks for signing me out, but why did you do it?" I asked.

"You're welcome," he said, then removed a black-looking thing from his pocket and pointed it at the prettiest truck I had ever seen in my life and pushed a button. The remote control disengaged the alarm on the late-model Range Rover.

"Is that your truck?"

"Yep."

"Man, I'm riding home in style," I said with a wide smile. "You're sure you ain't flipping those thangs, Mr. P?"

He stopped and stared at me. He didn't smile, and he didn't seem angry either, but I knew I had said the wrong thing. His brown eyes squinted as if he was trying to see through my forehead and into my brain.

"I want you to stop associating nice things with selling drugs," he said. "Okay?"

"The only people I know with nice things sell drugs, Mr. P. But I hear ya," I said before opening the passenger-side door. I sat down, and even through my jeans the leather seats were scorching hot.

"Put your seat belt on," Mr. P said as he hit a button, turning the vehicle on and blasting the air conditioner.

I ran my hands along the soft, leather-covered captain's chairs, then across the smooth wood grain on the dash. I had to get me one of these. This had officially become my dream car.

Mr. P stared at me and smiled.

My antennae went up. *What the heck is he smiling at? If this man tries something with me, I am going right back to jail for assault on a freak.* "What's wrong with you?"

"Nothing."

"Whatchu smiling for?"

"Because I feel like it," he said. "I can't smile in my own car?"

"I'm just saying."

"Saying what?" he asked, still smiling at me.

"What do you do for a living?" I asked.

"I run a nonprofit organization and I come up here and hang out with the likes of you."

"Driving this," I said, still looking around the sport utility vehicle in amazement. "Somebody's making a nice profit somewhere, and I thought you were a volunteer up here. I didn't know you got paid for that."

"I don't get paid, but that doesn't mean I don't do this for a living. I like working with you guys."

"Why?"

"Lord knows I wish I knew," he said, shaking his head.

I inhaled the cold air into my lungs, still watching Mr. P out of the corner of my eye. Then I felt guilty. This man had never given me any reason to believe he would harm a fly, yet I couldn't help but be distrustful of people who claimed to do things out of the kindness of their hearts.

"Where am I going?" he asked.

"You taking me home?"

"Where do you think I'm taking you, boy?"

"My bad. I live in the Bluff," I said. "You ever heard of the Bluff, Mr. P?"

"Yep," he said as he backed out of the parking lot and drove to the main street. "I'm very familiar with Vine City and the Bluff. I used to work with a few kids who lived over there."

"Who?"

He called out some names that I didn't know.

"So you know my hood, huh?"

"Not really. I just know where it is."

"I don't believe that. Something tells me you know these streets, Mr. P," I said, smiling. "You got a lil thugness 'bout cha."

Mr. P shook his head. "I used to be a street guy. Stealing cars, robbing folks, snatching purses. All kinds of ignorance, but that's not something to be proud of. As a matter of fact, it's something to be ashamed of. Being a criminal is stupid. It's a setup. You never get away and you can attest to that, Mr. I've-Been-Locked-Up-Thirty-Two-Times. These dumb rappers got y'all youngsters out here thinking jail is some kind of rite of passage or something, when in reality you're modern-day slaves."

"Mr. P, why you so hard on rappers?"

"I'm not hard on rappers. I just call it like I see it. Most of them are worse than the Ku Klux Klan. Sellouts. They get paid to spit ignorance and you buy into it, get locked up, and the folks who own the prisons get paid. The little white and Asian kids who would be competing with you for a job no longer have to worry about you. Why? Because you were more interested in being cool and hanging out than studying. Even if you don't have a criminal record, you're not prepared. Thank God that gangster rap is dying out. I don't even let my son listen to some radio stations."

"Why? It's just music."

"Nope. It's more than music. It's poison. Mental poison," he said.

"Is it really that deep, Mr. P?"

"Why did you put a tattoo on your face?"

"Because I like it," I said, not really feeling like going into the real reason I used my face as a canvas.

"And that's your final answer?" he said with a smile. "Because you like it? You're not in a position to do what you like right now. Lil Wayne can do whatever he wants with his face because he may never need a job. But you, on the other hand, will probably need one, and when you get a job you represent that company. Ever thought about that?"

I shook my head, but I wasn't trying to hear his preaching about something that wouldn't apply to me. I wasn't interested in getting a job. I was going to open up my own tattoo shop.

"Are you hungry?" Mr. P asked me. "I'm starving."

"I could go for a bite to eat."

"Whatcha want?"

"McDonald's will do."

"Man," he said, fanning me off. "That stuff isn't good for ya. You ever had Japanese?"

"Nope," I said. "I had Chinese."

"Well, let's tickle your taste buds a little bit," he said as his eyes darted to the navigation system. A picture of a telephone popped on and off of the screen. "Just a second, DeMarco."

He pushed a button and the radio went off. A female voice came through the car's speakers so clear it seemed like she was sitting in the backseat.

"Hey there," the woman said. "Where are you?"

"I'm just leaving the center. I have a wonderful young man in the car with me who has a tattoo on his face," Mr. P said.

"Hello, young man with a tattoo on his face," she said, and I immediately knew I would like her. There was something about her voice that let me know she was a good person.

"Hello," I said.

"I'm going to take him to grab a bite to eat, then drop him off at his house," Mr. P said. "What's up?"

"Oh. I have a meeting and I was wondering if you could pick Blake up from practice," she said.

Mr. P glanced over at the clock and nodded. "Yeah. I can. Where are the girls?"

"Arielle is reading some book about vampires and Lyric is watching television."

"*Hannah Montana* again?" Mr. P said.

"You know it," she said.

"A'ight. I will see you shortly. I was going to take De-Marco to Benihana, but they are probably packed with the lunch crowd, and the coach will have a fit if he has to stay late with Blake. We'll figure something out."

"Okay," she said. "Well, he's welcome to join us for dinner tonight."

"I'll see what he has planned," he said. "Chat with ya shortly. Love ya."

"I love you too."

I stared at him and realized that I had never heard a man express his feelings so openly. And I had heard about that Benihana place he mentioned before but never thought I would eat there. I had to admit I was a little disappointed that we weren't going.

"Was that your wife?"

"Yep," he said.

"She got you sprung, huh?"

He looked at me and laughed. "I would hope so. Do you like Chick-fil-A?"

"Yeah," I said, even though I had never been there.

"I owe you a nice lunch, but I have to go and pick up my son from football practice."

"How old is your son?"

"He's sixteen, like you."

"I bet he's never been to the juvey, huh?"

"Nah," Mr. P said, shaking his head. "Do you play sports?"

"Yeah, I play basketball and football. I used to play baseball when I was little, but it's boring so I quit."

"What positions do you play with football and basketball?"

"Football, I play receiver and safety; basketball, I play point and shooting guard. I got major game, man. What position does your son play—quarterback?"

"No," he said. "He's a running back. Tailback to be exact."

"Private school?"

"Nope."

"Wow. I would expect you to have the best of everything."

"He goes to a good school and he likes it, so it's all good. How tall are you, DeMarco?"

"Six-two, maybe six-three. I'm not sure," I said. "I like playing ball, but I don't have dreams of playing in the NBA or nuttin' like that. I'd rather draw."

"Is that right," he said. "What grade are you in?"

"Tenth."

"What kind of student are you, Dee?"

"I get straight As, Mr. P. I'm no dummy."

"An honor-roll thug. I've seen it all," he said as he released the steering wheel and threw his hands up.

"Whatever," I said.

We rode the rest of the way to my house chatting about

this and that. We made plans to get together over the weekend. He said he was going to introduce me to his family and take me out to eat for my birthday, and I couldn't wait. I liked hanging out with Mr. P.

We stopped by the Chick-fil-A and I had one of the best chicken sandwiches I had ever tasted. I ordered the lemonade and it was so good I was upset when I finished. A few minutes later, we were back on the highway headed toward the Bluff. We pulled up to the apartment complex and two of the four buildings that made up our section were boarded up. The crackheads and other street folks had taken over the abandoned building behind ours for all of their unscrupulous activities. The scum of the Bluff, was the name my sister called the crackheads and other substance abusers. At any given time you were liable to hear gunshots followed by screams in either of the condemned buildings. I used to hang out in them all the time, but now I was thinking it was time to stay clear of them.

"This is it," I said as we pulled directly in front of my apartment. One of the windows in my mother's bedroom was up, and I could hear my little brother crying his little heart out.

"Somebody sounds like they need a little attention," Mr. P said.

"That's my little brother and he's probably hungry."

"Well, now that you're home, maybe you can feed him."

"Yeah," I said, not sure how I felt about being back home.

"Now that I know where you are," he said, "I will come scoop you up this Friday around five."

"Cool," I said, reaching over to shake his hand. "Thanks again for signing me out, Mr. P."

"My pleasure. Just make sure you don't go back," he said with an easy smile.

"Fa'sho," I said as I got out of my dream car and headed back to the nightmare that was my life.

# 2

# DeMarco

I let myself into our apartment and stood in the living room looking around at the complete mess that I called home. It was almost one o'clock in the afternoon yet the place was almost completely dark. I stepped over a pile of clothes that was sitting in the middle of the floor and made my way over to the window to let a little light into the place. I turned and noticed three big trash bags that were busting at the seams sitting by the kitchen door. Another pile of dirty clothes was in the kitchen sink and smelled as sour as some month-old milk. I sighed and shook my head.

I walked into the living room and turned on the small television that was sitting on top of an older floor model. The heat inside the apartment was worse than outside, so I walked over and lifted both windows to allow a little fresh air into the place.

"Mommy. Mommy. Mooooomyyyyy, I'm hungry," a little

voice called out as I looked in the open door to my mother's bedroom and saw my brother tug on the bedspread, trying to wake my inebriated mother. "I'm hungry."

My little brother, Devin, didn't even bother to look my way when I let myself in. I couldn't help but smile when I noticed how big he had gotten since the last time I saw him. He was wearing a pair of blue underwear with an action figure on them and nothing else. His hair was in a matted afro and he looked like he hadn't had a washcloth on his face in at least a month. Tears made their way down his chubby cheeks as he looked around the room, afraid to wake their mother. Even at three years old, he knew the consequences of waking the woman when she was on her "medicine."

I walked over and stopped at the doorway to my mother's bedroom. He looked at me and frowned, but then a hint of recognition registered on his face and he immediately stopped crying.

"What's up, lil buddy?" I said.

The sound of my voice must've confirmed what he was already thinking in his little head because he smiled and ran as fast as his chubby legs would allow him to and jumped up into my arms.

"Whoa," I said, grunting from his weight. "Whatcha crying for?"

"I'm hungry," he said with a frown as he wiped away his tears. "And Momma won't wake up."

"Yeah," I said as I rubbed his back to reassure him that everything was going to be okay. "Let her sleep. I'll find you something to eat."

I then turned my attention to the pitiful sight lying before me. My mother, Sophia Winslow, was sprawled out on the bed wearing a dirty T-shirt, panties with holes in them, and a pair of surprisingly clean socks. Her bony legs were covered with dark marks from God knows where, and her hair looked like it hadn't been washed or curled in forever. She wore a frown on her skinny face even as she slept.

The fan against the wall was only circulating hot air around the already stuffy house.

I stared at the woman who gave me life and couldn't bring myself to even act like I cared about her. She was a mess and didn't care about anything or anybody. Once she had her hands on a bottle of liquor, everything and everybody could kick rocks.

But as I got older, I started to understand her a little better and the hate I once felt for her was replaced with pity. I used to hate her because she acted like she hated me, but, for whatever reason, I didn't hold anything against her anymore. Maybe I was getting soft in my old age, or perhaps all of those books that I read on alcoholism were paying off and I realized that she was sick. Sophia was a woman who got caught up in ghetto life and tried to escape through a bottle.

As I stood there staring at her, I tried to calculate her weight. She couldn't have been more than ninety-five pounds, and on a five-feet-seven-inch frame, that wasn't cute. Sophia gave birth to me and my twin sister, Jasmine, when she was fifteen years old, and the sad part about that was we weren't her first. Our oldest sister, Nicole, lived with her dad and hardly ever came around. She used to

show her face during the Thanksgiving or Christmas holi-
days, but a few years ago, even those visits stopped alto-
gether. I didn't blame her one bit. Nobody in their right
mind would want to live where we lived. Anybody who
ever said it's all good in the hood never lived in the Bluff.

"So let's see what we can get you to eat up in
this piece," I said as I carried my little brother to the
kitchen.

I flipped on the light switch and the roaches scattered
everywhere. We walked over to the refrigerator and before
I opened it I already knew what I would find, but I looked
anyway. The four hundred dollars a month in food vouch-
ers that the government gave to my mom was never used
for food. Sophia's happiest days of the month were the
first and fifteenth, when the welfare check came and the
EBT food-stamp card was filled with money. Those two
days seemed to be the only times she was happy. She always danced around the house like it was Christmas because she knew she would have a great high coming later
that night.

I closed the refrigerator and opened up the cabinets.
Nothing there either.

"We'll have to go get you something, buddy. This spot is
foodless."

"Okay," Devin said, burying his face in the side of my
neck.

We walked over to my sister Jasmine's bedroom and
knocked on the door, which was always closed.

No answer.

I turned the knob and opened the door. The yellow
and white comforter was neatly made and all of a gazillion

stuffed animals were seated in their usual positions. Her room was as neat and clean as ever. The walls were covered with Chris Brown and Trey Songz posters. The room looked as if it belonged in another house. Realizing she wasn't in there, I closed the door and walked back into the living room.

I tripped over a pair of men's boots and kicked them out of my way. I placed Devin down on our ridiculously nasty sofa. The thing needed to be placed out on the curb with the garbage because it looked as if someone had poured dirty car oil on it, then rubbed it in for good measure. I rubbed both of my temples to help me relax a little. I wasn't sure why I was feeling so overwhelmed and disgusted with the place I had called home for the last ten years.

I frowned at the smell of something that a breeze sent through the apartment.

"What the heck?" I said as I walked into the bathroom and covered my nose. The bathtub was filled with more dirty clothes, but that wasn't the source of the putrid smell. I looked in the toilet, and it was filled with something that needed to be in the sewer. I pushed the handle to flush but nothing happened. I walked out of the bathroom and closed the door behind me.

"Okay," I said as I walked back into the living room and picked up my little brother. "Let's get you on some clothes so we can get out of here. This place stinks and I'm about to get sick."

All of a sudden I wished I was back at the juvey center. I hated this place and everything about it. The Vine City (the Bluff) area of Atlanta is one of the poorest places you could live in the city, and violence and despair were the norm. I never thought too much about life outside of the Bluff—it's all I've ever known—but there was something growing inside of me that said I didn't belong here. Subconsciously, I knew a long time ago that I didn't belong here, even if leaving meant going to jail. When I was younger and life in the Bluff got to be too much, I would commit a petty crime just to get sent to juvenile hall. Even though it was jail, it was ten times better than my home life. At least I was guaranteed three hot meals, a shower, and a place to sleep. The trade-off had always worked out in my favor, and most of the time when my release date came up, I wasn't happy about it.

"Who dat out there?" my mother said.

I didn't respond. I was too busy rummaging through the pile of clothes trying to find a decent shirt and shorts for my little brother.

Sophia's bony body appeared in the doorway and staggered. She held on to the wall and stared at me.

"When you get home?" she said as if she really didn't care what my answer would be.

I ignored her and continued going through the clothes. I could've been home three weeks sooner if she would've just gotten her lazy butt on a MARTA bus and come to sign me out.

"Oh, you turned deaf?" she said as she turned around and walked back into her bedroom.

"Let's get some clothes on ya, fella," I said as I found a shirt and shorts that looked like they would fit. I put the clothes on Devin. "Go and put on your shoes, man."

Devin jumped off the sofa and ran into their mother's bedroom. A few seconds later he came back holding a dirty pair of off-brand shoes. He sat on the floor and slipped his sockless feet into his shoes.

"Where is Jasmine, man?" I asked Devin.

"She gone," he said.

"Gone where?"

"I don't know," he said.

"DeMarco," Sophia called from her bedroom. "Bring some cigarettes from the store."

*Yeah, you wait on 'em,* I thought.

"Was she here this morning?" I asked.

"No," he said, shaking his little head. "She left last night."

I nodded my head and added that to the list of things I needed to check out. I had been hearing some very troubling rumors about Jasmine and I wasn't very happy about it. I reached down and picked up Devin and carried him to the bathroom. I opened the door, smelled the stench, then closed it back.

"We'll wash your face in the kitchen, man," I said.

The roaches were really bothering me. I sat Devin on the counter and stepped on as many of the little creatures as I could before giving up. I grabbed a dishcloth from the towel rack and turned on the faucet. The rusty sink had seen better days and the water was a slow trickle. Once the cloth was wet enough, I cleaned my little brother up as best I could.

"Are ya ready, birthday big guy?" I said. I always thought it was cool that Devin shared the same birthday as me and Jasmine.

"Yes," he said as if he didn't even know that today was his special day. "Can I have some cake and balloons?"

"Of course you can. What would a birthday be without cake and balloons," I said, then reached out and tickled his stomach.

# 3

## DeMarco

I walked out of the stifling hot apartment with Devin on my heels. Georgia had been experiencing a slight heat wave, but I had escaped most of it because the juvey center kept the air conditioner on full blast twenty-four hours a day. It was four o'clock in the afternoon and the temperatures were in the high nineties. Summers in the ghetto were brutal. Tempers were short and people who were running around in the springtime were often six feet below the earth's surface before the summer was over.

Devin reached up for me to carry him, so I reached down and scooped him up. "Now, you're getting too big to be carrying around, fella," I said as I lifted him up. "But since it's your birthday, I'll make an exception."

"My birthday?" Devin asked.

"Yep. You're three years old today. Show me three fingers?"

Devin held up his fingers and smiled.

"That's how old you are. You're getting to be an old man."

He smiled and his eyes lit up.

"Guess what?"

"What?"

"Today is my birthday too," I said. "And Jasmine's."

"Is it the birthday for everybody?" he asked, wide-eyed. "Mommy's too?"

"No," I said. "Not Mommy's. Just me, you, and Jaz's. I know you want cake and balloons, but what else do you want to do to celebrate your day, dude?"

"Eat cake and hot dogs, then play with some balloons," he said.

"That's it?"

Devin nodded his head and smiled with his chubby cheeks.

"Well, I figured eating would be in there somewhere. But we're gonna have some real fun. How about we play some video games, eat some pizza, and get a cake. We can even go to Dave and Buster's and let you play with the rich kids."

"What is Dave and Buster's?"

I smiled and turned my head just in time to see my homeboy Melvin "Jolly" Harris riding up on a bike that was way too small for his wide frame. Jolly was tall and fat. He was fifteen years old and already six feet three inches tall, but he was also close to three hundred pounds. Football coaches practically begged him to play, but he was lazy and couldn't last more than a few days of workouts.

"Hey, boy," Jolly yelled, loud enough for the people three streets over to hear him. "You home?"

"Nah, brainiac," I said. "It's just your imagination."

"You always tryna get smart with somebody, Dee. I should hop off this bike and choke you out."

"You should hop off that bike and give those tires a rest."

"Oh, I see you got jokes."

We slapped hands and Jolly reached out to give Devin a high five.

"So what's the plan now that you home?" he asked.

"Hopefully I can stay out this time. I'm tired of that crap, man."

"Yeah," Jolly said, having been where I just left more times than he cared to count. "Things changing round here, man. Look over there."

Jolly pointed to a white woman who was watering some plants in the front yard of a house that was abandoned when I left the neighborhood seven months ago but was now totally renovated. The old ranch-style house used to have busted-out windows and spray paint all over the outer walls and was pretty much used as a crack house. Now the place looked like it belonged in some fancy magazine. The house sported expensive-looking windows, freshly painted walls, a big red door, and a new roof. There was a black wrought-iron fence around the house, which made it stick out like a sore thumb in our desolate community.

"That's weird. Why would she want to buy that house in this neighborhood?" I asked as I stared at the woman.

"Don't know, but I'll tell you this. Nobody will touch her, bro. You try to rob that white woman and the police will be on you so fast that your head will spin. You won't even go to jail 'cause them white boys taking you straight to the chair," Jolly said, shaking his fat head from side to side. "We can kill each other all day long, but that one dere? No, sir. Off-limits, player."

"I see," I said as I looked down the block at a few more houses. All of them had FOR SALE signs in the yards and most of the signs were marked SOLD. I guess they too would soon experience a similar transformation.

"Your gear is a mess, player," Jolly said, looking down at my too-small shoes and high-water pants. "You looking like a tatted-up Steve Urkel round here."

"Yeah," I said. "These shoes are killing my feet. I need to go shopping, but they are all I have for now, so I gotta deal with it."

"And those pants are killing my eyes," Jolly said as he leaned down and moved some imaginary dirt from his fresh pair of Air Jordans. He was wearing the biggest pair of Polo khaki shorts that I had ever seen and a Hollister T-shirt. He handed me a cell phone. "Here ya go, playboy."

"I forgot all about this thing," I said as I reached out to grab my old phone. "You just walk around with my phone?"

"Nah, fool, I saw you out of my window. A thank-you would be nice."

"Thanks, bro."

"I need to get me another tat. When can you hook me up?"

"Whenever you have your money right," I said, pushing the buttons to the cell phone. "Is it still on?"

"Yep. I paid it for ya," Jolly said with a wide-gap, toothy smile.

"How much do I owe you?"

"You straight. It wasn't but 'bout twenty or thirty dollars a month. No big deal, playa."

"I'll take that off of whatever I charge you for your tattoo."

"Man," he said, fanning me off and pulling out a wad of money and waving it in my face. "Do I look like I'm hurting?"

"Not at all," I said, surprised to see my best friend with so much money.

Jolly was always poorer than the rest of the kids in the area, and that wasn't saying much because none of us ever had more than two good pennies to rub together. Now the fact that he was standing in front of me wearing fresh clothes, two-hundred dollar sneakers, and waving around wads of cash concerned me.

"Well, a'ight then," he said, pulling out another stack from his other pocket and sniffing both rolls of money. "Aww, the sweet smell of cheese. So when can I come by?"

"Tomorrow around five. I need to go get some supplies after I come home from school," I said, giving him a look that said I didn't approve.

"It ain't even that, player," he said, reading my mind. "I got a job. A real job."

"Doing what?"

"Painting houses with my uncle. I get paid ten dollars an hour and I've been working all summer, player. Selling drugs is for handicaps. I got too many skills to be getting jacked like that."

"So why don't you get a bank account instead of walking around with your money, showing it off. You know you can't fight."

"You crazy. I got them hands, boy. Fool must've lost his mind if he tries to take mine's. Left the .45, but I keeps the nine," he rapped, then held up his shirt to expose the handle of a gun.

"Looks like the tools of a painter," I said with a chuckle. "I don't know who you think you're fooling with that paint lie, but that's your choice."

"Six feet three"—Jolly started with a makeshift mike to his mouth as he ignored me—"Sexy as can be. Girls see me, and pee pee, and beg me please. Take me to the hotel, Jolly, they say. I be like, naw not today, I'm on my way to the . . ."

"Please, shut up," I said, not even interested in hearing the latest creation of his whackness.

"Keep sleeping on the skills, player. I'ma 'bout to blow, and you gonna be the main one talking 'bout can I go on tour with you."

"Have you seen Jasmine?" I asked, changing the subject.

Jolly, who always could be found cheesing from ear to ear, changed his facial expression immediately. He dropped his head and took a deep breath.

"Is that a yes or no?" I asked.

"That's a yes and a no, player," he said. "I haven't seen the Jasmine I know in a minute now. But last night I saw her. She was riding around in a brand-new truck with them leeches she calls friends. I'm surprised all of them ain't locked up."

"Who? Riding around with who?" I asked, anxious for an answer.

"As a matter of fact, we were standing right where me and you standing at right now when I asked what she was doing with those leeches. She cussed me out and told me to mind my business, so that's what I did."

"What girls are you talking about, Jolly?" I asked with a frown.

Jolly shook his head as if what he was about to say was too much. "They call themselves the Divas. It's three of them. Kecia and Tiny and some fat chick. They be out here hooking up with older cats and getting 'em for that paper. They hitting up stores for high-price purses and selling them to some white woman who comes through in a fancy car. Now Jaz rolling with them. She too smart for that life, bro. I always knew Jaz was gonna be the one who made it outta here. Broke my heart to see her with them clowns, player. And I ain't seen her in school in a few days. I hope she hasn't dropped out."

My heart hit the ground and I had to force myself not to blow my lid. I took a couple of deep breaths to calm my nerves.

"A'ight," I said as I reached out to tap fist. "Come see me tomorrow around five and I'll hook that tat up for ya."

"Cool," Jolly said. "What y'all 'bout to do?"

"I need to run in here and pick up a few things for the house, and then I'ma take Devin to Dave and Buster's for his birthday."

"What? Today is lil man's birthday?" Jolly said as he reached into his pocket. He pulled out a five-dollar bill and handed it to Devin. "Happy birthday, lil buddy. Buy yourself some candy, on me."

"Okay," Devin said, taking the money.

"What do you say, Devin?" I said.

"Thank you," he replied.

"You straight," Jolly said. "A'ight, Dee. I'ma holla at cha later. I gotta go handle a lil business."

"Why aren't you in school?"

"I wasn't feeling too good this morning, so I slept in," he said. I knew right away he was lying, and I let him know it by twisting my lip.

"For real," he said, sticking to his lie.

"I hear ya," I said. I had seen so many of my friends cross over into the land of drug selling and street life. When you grew up as poor as we were, more people crossed over than stayed on the straight and narrow. I wasn't going to be one of them. I was concerned about Jolly, but I couldn't afford to worry about him right now.

Devin and I walked into the neighborhood corner store, and the bell above the door alerted the owner of our presence.

"How you doing, Mrs. Gloria?" I said.

"Hey, baby," the old woman said with a wide smile. Mrs. Gloria had to be at least seventy-five years old, and she had been a godsend to us ghetto children. The old lady was still pretty and vibrant. She had long white hair flowing down her back, giving away her Indian heritage. She had been running this store with her husband, Mr. Mason, for the last fifty years. "You sure that ain't your son instead of your lil brother?"

"That would put me at thirteen years old when he was born, twelve when he was conceived, so I'm pretty sure I'm not the pappy," I said.

"Y'all look just alike. I haven't seen you in a while. Where you been, locked up again?"

"Yep," I said as I picked up a handbasket and walked down an aisle.

"When are you gonna stay out of trouble long enough to help get yo momma straight? Seems to me like she's getting worse."

"Yeah," I said, then tried to change the subject. "How is Mr. Mason doing?"

"He's not doing too good. I had to put him in a care center. It broke my heart, but I couldn't lift him up no more."

"I'm sorry to hear that. Where is he? I'll drop by and see him."

"He's way out there in Conyers. That's in Rockdale County, but save your trip. He won't know who you are. Alzheimer's done got the best of him," she said, shaking her head and taking a deep breath. "It's in God's hands, so I just try to support him as best I can."

"I'm sorry to hear that, Mrs. Gloria. Tell him I asked about him."

"I'll tell him but . . . ," she said, then shook her head, but just as fast she perked back up. "You know your sister is looking real good these days, which means she doing something real bad."

That got my attention.

Mrs. Gloria shook her head as if her mind was roaming over the many lives she saw ruined as they fell prey to the Bluff.

"So I hear," I said. "When was the last time you seen her?"

"Last night. She came in here talking all loud, showing out for them girls she's running around with," Mrs. Gloria said with her lips twisted. "I had to get her straight because she must've lost her mind for a minute."

I didn't like the sound of that. One of the things that Jasmine had always taken pride in was the way she carried herself, especially around her elders.

"Go on and get what you need. Your momma ain't been

in here this month, so that means she done sold her food-stamp card. But children shouldn't starve just 'cause they parents don't have the sense God gave them. Go on and get what you need."

"I have money," I said proudly. For as long as I could remember, me and my family had always had hand-me-downs, and I hated it. I wanted to have my own, like the kids I saw on television or some of the kids at school. Once I realized how much people were paying for tattoos, I started charging, and this last stay in the juvey, I made over three hundred dollars. I could've quadrupled that if I was on the street.

"Did I ask you if you had your own money?" Mrs. Gloria snapped. "Save your lil money. As a matter of fact, where did you get money from? Unless they started paying folks to go to jail?"

"I work."

"Yeah, I bet you work. Doing what?"

"Art," I said proudly.

"Humph," she said, fanning me off. "Anyway, I had a distributor who dropped off too much stuff and didn't charge me for it. My books coming up off balance."

I looked around the store for something to lessen my little brother's hunger pangs. I knew she was lying about the distributor dropping off too much stuff, but that was Mrs. Gloria. She loved the kids of the Bluff. Word around town was that she had a huge house out in Stone Mountain or someplace, but she spent most of her time with us in the hood. I walked around the store and picked up two packs of bacon, two pounds of ground beef, a dozen eggs, a box of pancake mix, a gallon of orange juice, a loaf of bread, some cookies, one gallon of milk, a box of Cap'n

Crunch cereal, some Lysol surface cleaner, and a can of Raid bug spray. I placed the items on the counter and looked down at my little brother, who had found a toy car and was down on his hands and knees zooming it around the floor. "Get up from down there, boy. That floor is dirty."

"Let that baby play," Mrs. Gloria snapped at me. "That floor ain't no dirtier than the one Sophia keep at y'all house. I went over there the other day and almost passed out from the smell."

I didn't respond, but her words didn't sit too well with me. I knew the old lady didn't mean any harm by her comment, but it still stung. I placed a twenty-dollar bill on the counter.

"Didn't I just tell you to keep your money," she said.

I hunched my shoulders. "I'd rather pay."

Mrs. Gloria pulled on her long ponytail, which was hanging over the front of her shoulder, and huffed. "Suit yourself," she said and started ringing up the items. "Twenty-eight dollars and thirty-one cent."

I went into my pockets and pulled out a ten-dollar bill and handed it to her. "How much is that car he's playing with?"

"It's free," she said with a mean scowl on her face. "Just because you got a little bit of money, you think you can come up in here and offend me, boy?"

"Okay, okay, okay," I said with my disarming smile. "Today is his birthday. Tell Mrs. Gloria thank you for the car, Devin."

"Thank you, Mrs. Gloria," Devin said without looking up.

"Oh, really," she said, pushing my money back toward me. "That means it's your birthday too. And I don't take

money on birthdays. Consider this a birthday gift to all of
y'all. I don't know how Sophia managed to have three
kids on the same day."

"I'm sure it wasn't planned," I said.

"Y'all go on and get out of here," Mrs. Gloria said.

"Thank you, Mrs. Gloria," I said as I bagged my items.
"You have a good day."

"You too, and stay your lil tail out of jail. And I'm so sad
to see that you messed with God's creation by putting
them ugly drawings on your face."

I threw my hand up and waved good-bye. We walked
out of the store and back out into the heat wave. As we
made our way down the street, we passed ten or fifteen
older guys who were slumped over in front of the check-
cashing place shooting dice. They were talking loud as
they threw the little white stones against the wall.

"What's up, Dee," one of the guys who was looking on
said.

"Wassup," I said as we walked past.

"I need to get me a tat, boy," another one said.

"You know where to find me."

"How much?"

"We'll work it out," I said as we kept on moving down
the street.

We turned the corner and the new white lady was still
out in her yard working. She looked our way and smiled.

"Hi there, Mr. Devin," she said as she walked over to
her tall gate.

"Hey, Mrs. Burger," Devin said.

The white woman smiled and shook her head. "Who
are you with today, Master Devin?"

"I'm Devin's brother, DeMarco. Nice to meet you."

She looked at me and did a double take as if she was sizing me up as a friend or foe.

"Nice house," I said.

"It's nice to meet you too," she said with a smile showing off the whitest teeth I had ever seen. She had to be in her late forties or early fifties, but her teeth looked like they belonged in the mouth of a twenty-year-old. "You know that I just absolutely adore this young man."

Devin held up his toy car and waved it as if to say *look what I have*.

She leaned down and removed her gloves from her pale hands, then stuck one through the wrought-iron bars and pinched Devin on his cheek. "Aren't you the cutest little fella."

"Today is my birthday," Devin said.

"Oh, really," she said in mock surprise. "How old are you?"

"Three," Devin said, holding up his fingers.

"Well, I will have to see if I can't do something special for you. After all, you only turn three once."

Devin smiled and looked up at me. He was getting used to this birthday thing.

"I'm Michelle Eichelberger," she said, standing up and extending her hand to me.

"DeMarco Winslow," I said, shaking her hand.

"It's nice to meet you, DeMarco," she said with a wide, welcoming smile. "I'm surprised that I haven't seen you around. I see this little guy every day."

"I just got home," I said.

"Were you away on a summer vacation?"

"I guess you can say that," I said with a smile. "Is your last name German?"

She nodded her head and looked at me as if she was surprised I recognized her country of origin. "It is. I moved to this country five years ago."

"How do you like it so far?"

She held her hand out and wiggled it from side to side. "So-so. It has its good and bad, but it's home now."

The group of guys who were shooting dice in front of the check-cashing place got rowdy and started arguing. Then someone pulled out a gun and let off a shot, sending the crowd scrambling in every direction.

The white woman jumped back and almost stumbled trying to get back into her house. Devin and I didn't even flinch.

"Well, let me get these groceries in the house. It was nice meeting you, Mrs. Eichelberger," I said casually.

"Oh my goodness," she said as she turned around and ran up her steps.

I wanted to laugh at the woman's panic because I was sure she didn't count on midday gunshots when she purchased her house. Devin and I continued on our way down the street to our apartment.

I could hear the yelling before we could even make it to the door. Sophia and Jasmine were standing in the living room screaming at each other at the top of their lungs.

"I ain't giving you jack," Jasmine said. "You better get your little liquor however you been getting it, and get out of my face."

"Who you think you're talking to?" Sophia pointed her finger at Jasmine, who was already a few inches taller than her.

"You," Jasmine said, standing her ground.

I looked at my sister as I walked between them. She

looked like a grown woman. Her hair was cut short like the singer Rihanna and her face was covered with makeup.

"Oh yeah?" Sophia said, still wearing her dirty T-shirt and hole-filled underwear. "I'll tell you what. Since you wanna talk all disrespectful, you can get your lil narrow tail out of my house. I don't know who you think you're talking to, girl, but I don't tolerate no back talk."

I walked into the kitchen and placed the bags on the counter. I ignored both of them and pulled out the can of bug spray. I started spraying the roaches and watched them die.

"Well, good afternoon to you too," Sophia said to me. "You can't speak either?"

"Hello," I said as I stopped spraying long enough to open the window.

"Hey, Dee," Jasmine said with a smile. "When you get home?"

"Not too long ago," I said, trying my best to give her the silent treatment.

"Okay," she said, trying to read my lack of communication with her. "That's what's up."

I continued spraying and she gave me a strange look, then walked into her bedroom and closed the door.

"Who signed you out?" Sophia asked me.

I ignored her and continued spraying the insects. I coughed a few times as the fumes got to be too much.

"Oh, so you done lost your hearing. This one lost her mind and you done lost your hearing. Where you get money for groceries?"

I stopped spraying and stared at the shell of a woman who stood before me. The hate I once felt was rising up again, so I took a deep breath and went back to what I was doing.

Sophia sucked her teeth and walked into the kitchen.

"Whatchu got in here to eat?"

I still didn't respond.

"You got a few dollars you can lend me until the first?"

"Nope," I said.

"Nope," she repeated as if I had better change the answer. "Whatchu mean, nope? I guess you spent all of your money on this food, huh?"

I opened up the cabinets and started spraying inside of them. There was a fan hanging from the middle of the ceiling and I pulled the string.

"What done got into you? You wanna be an exterminator now?" Sophia asked.

I ignored her once again and started putting away the groceries.

"Boy," she said, walking close to me. "You sure have gotten tall. How tall are you now?"

I was six feet two inches tall and had dark chocolate skin; Jasmine was almost six feet tall with the same complexion, but Sophia and Devin had light complexions.

"Can I have a hug?" she said with a raggedy smile that was in desperate need of a dentist. "I haven't seen you in a long time."

I stopped what I was doing and looked down at my mother. She looked pathetic. Life had really done a number on her. I leaned down and hugged her. She felt like a skeleton within my embrace and I immediately drew back.

She smiled. "I was gonna come and get you today, but I see they went on and let you out."

"Yep," I said.

"I'm going to take a nap. You need to talk to your sister 'bout that big mouth of hers. She gonna mess around and get the taste slapped out of it. And that ain't no lie."

Once again I ignored her.

Sophia turned and walked back into her bedroom.

After I put away the groceries, I walked to Jasmine's bedroom door and knocked.

# 4

## DeMarco

"Can I come in?" I said from outside my sister's bedroom door.

There was no answer, so I reached out and twisted the door handle. I slowly opened the door and saw her sitting on the bed with her head in her hands.

"What's up?" I said as I walked over and pulled the chair out from under her desk. I turned the chair around and took a seat across from her.

Jaz wiped her eyes and stared at me.

"I hate that woman," she said.

"You don't hate her; you just hate what she does."

She frowned at me and jerked her head back as if she wasn't expecting that response.

"What have you done to your hair, girl?" I asked, trying to ease the tension in the room.

She ran her fingers through her short hair. The last time I had seen her, it was long and her pride and joy. Now it was all gone. The sides were almost as short as mine, and the top part was sticking up in little spikes with pink tips.

"What did you do to your face?" she asked with a blank look.

"Just something to kill the boredom, plus I wanted to do something different," I said as I ran my own hand across my tattoo.

"You look like Mike Tyson," she said. "It's kind of cool though."

"Thanks," I said. "So what's been up, Jaz? I haven't seen you in a minute. No visits, no letters, nothing. I thought we were cool."

"We are cool," she said. "I don't know. I didn't think you would be gone that long."

"It's all good. I could've gotten out earlier, but your mom wouldn't come sign me out."

"So they just let you out, or did her sorry self come get you?"

"Nah," I said. "This dude who works there signed me out. A real good cat. I can't wait for you to meet him."

She nodded her head.

"I need to move my stuff," she said. "I'm not staying in this house with that woman one more night. I despise her and her ugly boyfriend."

"Boyfriend?"

"Yeah," Jasmine said. "Can you believe it? Well, once you meet him you'll believe it. He's a pathetic-looking something."

I didn't respond.

"He better keep his eyes on her and off me before I end up doing something to him."

"I'll take care of that. You don't have to move anywhere," I said.

"I'm not staying here with that woman. I hate her."

"No, you don't," he said. "Well, maybe you do, but you shouldn't. She's aggravating and she's annoying, but she's harmless. You just have to learn to ignore her."

"I don't even be here, and whenever I show up she starts cussing and asking me for money. Don't even ask where I been, how I'm doing. Nothing. Just wants money to get drunk with."

"Well, how are you doing?" I asked.

"I'm fine."

"Where have you been?"

"Staying with my friends."

"What friends?"

"Just friends."

"Jasmine," I said with a frown. "I'm older than you by seven minutes, so that means I'm your big bro."

"Whatever," she said, fanning me off.

"I'm serious," I said. "I'm hearing things."

"So what? That's all people do round here is talk. They need to mind their own business and stay out of mine."

"Jaz, this isn't you. I'm the one who gets in trouble, not you. You're supposed to be the smart one."

"I am smart, but I'm tired of living like some third-world citizen. I'm tired of having a drug addict slash alcoholic for a mother, and tired of her stupid boyfriend plotting for his chance to try me. I'm tired of being hungry because she uses the food card for liquor and whatever else she's doing. Then she has the nerve to ask me to give her money to stay here? Are you kidding me?"

"Yeah, but forget all of that. I'll take care of the food. What's up with this Diva business?"

Her face froze. Jasmine and I always kept it real with each other. Ever since we were old enough to think, we pretty much knew that we could only count on each other, so lies and games were out of the equation early.

"You gotta know where that will lead you. If you don't know, let me help you," I said. "Jail. Now I've decided that I've gone for the last time. No matter what, I'm going to do things different this time."

"I heard that before," she said, rolling her eyes.

"Okay. You don't have to believe me, but you'll see. I've been reading, studying, and thinking along different lines. I have talent and I'm gonna use that talent to put some food on our table. But the thing I don't think you realize, Jaz, is once those folks get you on their radar . . . they try their best to keep you there. Before you know it, you'll be in and out of those cells until you think life is better in one than it is out here."

Jasmine looked at me as if I were an alien or something. Any other time, I would be trying to find out how I could make a few bucks out of her Diva connection, but I was done with that street crap.

"What in the world has happened to my brother?"

I smiled. "Today's our birthday; I guess I'm growing up. I suggest you join me, or should I wait seven more minutes and holla back at you?"

Jasmine smiled too. She took a deep breath and exhaled. "I like that tattoo, Dee," she said as she reached out and touched my face. "Everybody's been coming around here looking for you to get their tats."

"Oh yeah," I said. "That's a good thing. I'm about to set up shop, but first things first."

"What?"

"You need to leave those girls alone. I'm going to school in the morning and you're coming with me."

"School? You? Oh my God," Jasmine said. "Mr. I'll make it three times a week. I'm trying to figure out who kidnapped my brother and brainwashed him."

"It's sad that when I talk about doing the right thing, you think I'm brainwashed."

"I'm just kidding, boy," she said. "What you do, join the Muslims or something? You on some real different stuff, but it's cool."

"Are you hungry?" I asked.

"Nah. I'm straight," she said. "Me and Momma finally agreed on one thing. She wants me out and I don't want to be here. So I need to pack my things because I'm leaving."

"You're not going anywhere, so take a nap and calm down. I'm home now, and I promise you things will be different. That little boyfriend of hers will be dealt with. Trust me on that."

"I ain't worried about that bum. Trust me, he ain't crazy. Plus he ain't worth you going back to juvey over."

"I hear ya. Devin is hungry, so I'm about to cook a lil something. Then I'ma take him out to this place called Dave and Buster's so he can have some fun. Why don't you come with us?"

"I can't," Jasmine said.

"Why?"

"I have something to do."

"I haven't seen you in six months. Is what you have to

do more important than spending your birthday with your brothers?"

"I don't know. I gotta take care of some things."

"And you can't do it another time?"

Jasmine looked away and shook her head. I stared at my sister and couldn't help but wonder what was really going on in her world.

# 5

## JASMINE

I laid my head on my bed and thought back to how I had gotten myself to where I was. And to be honest, I wasn't sure where I was, but for the first time in my life, I felt good about myself. It's funny how life can sometimes throw you a curve ball that seems unhittable, but somehow, some way, you rear back and take a swing at it and knock the ball beyond the fence.

My life had been turned completely upside down over the last week, and that was a good thing. I went from being just another dirty, hungry little girl in the Bluff to looking like a million bucks. For the first time in my life, I liked me. I liked who I saw staring back at me in the mirror, and even though I knew that when things seemed too good to be true, more than likely the bottom would eventually fall out, I was willing to take that chance, and it all started because my mother's boyfriend was trying to get himself stabbed. I thought back to how it all got started.

I had to pull a knife on Sophia's pedophile boyfriend because he kept crossing the line with me. For the life of me, I can't understand how some women will choose the companionship of some sorry dude over the safety of their own child. I was going to go over to my grandmother's house, but my uncle Moochie was staying over there and he was crazy. The man was forty-three years old and still trying to be a rapper. All he did every day was sit in front of the television watching bootlegged DVDs, drink his beer, and write raps in his notepad. He was annoying as anybody could ever be, so going over there was not looking like a good option for me. Plus Granny's house reeked of urine. My grandmother was only sixty-seven years old, but she had kidney problems and had problems controlling her bladder, so the doctor had her wear adult diapers. But Uncle Moochie didn't change the things like he should, so she sat around all day smelling like crap. Granny was a big woman and I knew I couldn't lift her, so I would either have to put up with the smell or stay fighting with Uncle Moochie as I tried to get him to change her. The more I thought about it, the more I realized that Granny's house would only be used as a last resort.

These thoughts were racking my brain as I stood there going back and forth with my mother.

*"You better tell your man to keep his eyes in his head and off of me,"* I said as I walked out of the bathroom wrapped in a paper-thin towel that had seen better days.

*"Oh hush, Jasmine,"* Sophia said, fanning me away as if I was a nuisance. *"Otis ain't paying you no kind of attention, girl. What the heck he wanna look at you for? He has a woman right here. A real woman. Not some bigmouth lil girl who think she's grown. Get over yourself."*

*"I don't know what he wants to look at me for, but he knew I was in the shower and he walked in there anyway. Then he pulled the shower curtain back," I said. "I guess he's deaf and just didn't hear the shower running."*

*"Stop lying," Sophia shouted. "You just close your lying mouth, girl."*

*"I don't have to lie on that old ugly bastard," I said as I felt myself become livid with disgust.*

*"Otis a good man, and you're just trying to mess things up for me. You're so selfish that you just can't stand to see me happy."*

*"Happy? Yeah, okay," I said, shaking my head at this entire scene. "You go on and be happy, but if he tries that mess again, I'm gonna make him wish he made a better choice."*

*She stood there staring at me as if I were the world's biggest liar.*

*"Just tell him to stay out of the bathroom when I'm in there," I said as I walked back to my bedroom.*

*"You don't have any rooms around here. This my house," she said, and placed a hand on her bony hip.*

*I stopped and turned around and stared at the woman who I used to call my mother. "I don't even know why I'm talking to you. You care more about your liquor and that sorry waste of human life that you call your man, than you do your own kids."*

*"Kids? I got one kid. I got three wannabe grown-ups, so I don't know what you're talking about. Nicole don't come around, you know everything and half of what you think you know is a lie, and your brother wanna be a criminal. So far as I'm concerned, I don't have to worry 'bout nobody but Devin."*

"You're pathetic," I said. "And I don't blame Nicole. Who would want to stay around you if they had someplace else to go?"

"Well, why don't you find someplace else to go?" she said, and turned on her heels and walked back to her room.

"I will, and I'll make sure to call down to the welfare office and tell them that I don't live here anymore. And I'll tell them that DeMarco hasn't been here either. Let's see how you get your money for your liquor then."

The threat to her liquor sent her into a rage. She turned around and ran at me as if she were going to attack me. But she knew better. The mother-daughter dynamic had changed years ago. We merely existed in the same house. I hated her and she hated me.

"You better keep them white folks out of my business, girl. Because if I get one visit, I swear before God that you will wish you never knew how to pick up a phone. And you can take that to the bank."

"You don't scare me," I said as I walked up to her. I towered over her, and for the first time in my life I saw some fear in my mother's face. "You keep your filthy, disgusting-looking man out of my face and out of the bathroom while I'm in there. If he says one more word to me, I'm calling the cops on him and you. Now you take that to the bank."

"Oh, so you think you bad now, huh?" she said as she looked up at me. "Okay. Well, there is only one bad mamma jamma in this place, and that's me. So get your crap and hit the road."

"Nah," Otis said, as he walked in with a smile on his

face. "Let her stay here. She's just a teenager. Leave her alone."

I stared back at him and he gave me a wink. I calmly walked past him and into the kitchen. I went over to the utensil drawer and pulled out a steak knife. I turned around and walked up to him.

"Whatchu gonna do with that?" he said with a smile.

"If you ever say one more word to me, I'm going to put this in your eyes."

"Okay," he said with a smile. "I love you too, Jasmine."

"I will end your days right now if you ever think about putting your filthy hands on me. Do you hear me?"

"I hear ya, baby," Otis said as if this whole conversation was amusing him.

I wanted to stab that man right in his ugly face, but he wasn't worth me going to jail.

"Get out," Sophia said. "Get your stuff and get out."

I kept my eyes on Otis. He was ugly; black as a car tire, raggedy beard, and hair that hadn't been groomed in ages. Then he had the audacity to be short. He wasn't even five-feet-three-inches tall. I couldn't stand the sight of him or my so-called mother, so I lowered the knife and backed away from the two nutcases.

I went to my room, gathered me a few items, and threw them in my big Nike gym bag. I wasn't sure where I was going, but I knew staying with Sophia, the alcoholic, and her pedophile boyfriend was no longer an option.

Once I had my things in my bag, I walked out into the living room and saw my little brother, Devin. He was sitting on the dirty floor watching the old raggedy television set. I leaned down and picked him up.

"Hey, buddy," I said as I wiped away the tears from my

*eyes. I hated to leave him with this poor excuse for a mother, but I was going to have my hands full making my own way. I couldn't imagine trying to take care of a rambunctious three-year-old.*

*"Where you going?" Devin asked me as he looked at my gym bag, which was busting at the seams.*

*"I'm not sure," I said. "Maybe over to a friend's for a few days. I don't know."*

*"Can I go?" he asked.*

*"No, but I will come back over and check on you tomorrow," I said.*

*He turned his little lips upside down and folded his arms in protest to my answer. He knew who fed, clothed, and bathed him, and it wasn't Sophia.*

*"I'll be back over here tomorrow," I said as I looked at Sophia's closed bedroom door.*

*"I'm hungry," he said.*

*"No, you're not," I said. "I just got you something to eat thirty minutes ago."*

*"Uh-huh," he said, nodding his head. "I am."*

*I sat him back down on the floor. "Don't fall asleep on that floor. Get on the sofa."*

*"Okay," he said.*

I shook the thoughts from my head, grabbed my bag and walked out of the house. I stood on the front steps, trying to decide what I was going to do. That's when Kecia, Tiny, and Shemika pulled up in a brand-new, pearl-white Cadillac Escalade.

"What's up, Jaz?" Kecia said. "You wanna roll with us? We 'bout to go have some fun."

I stood there thinking of my options. Grandma's house wasn't very appealing, and living with my mother was even less. I could deal with the drinking, the cursing, the filthy apartment, but I drew the line when she called me a liar in favor of her sorry excuse for a man. I had already started staying away from the apartment more and more, and when I was there, I placed a chair on my door handle to reinforce the lock at night just to feel safe.

"Whatcha gonna do, girl? We ain't got all night," Kecia said. "And what's up with the gym bag?"

I didn't even need to respond. I just frowned and jerked my hand toward my house, and she immediately knew why I was out there.

"Come on and roll with us," Kecia said excitedly as she bounced behind the wheel of the brand-new car.

Kecia Harrison was my friend since we were knee-high to a mosquito. We met back when we were four or five years old, running around playing hopscotch in the streets. She always was treated with disdain by the other ghetto children, who couldn't wait to take out their life's frustrations on another poor soul. Kecia was an easy target because she was super skinny, and even at a young age had bad skin. Needless to say, her self-esteem was pretty low. Now, at sixteen, she was still skin and bones and her acne had somehow gotten worse. She was exactly the type of person Tiny needed in her crew.

Tiny Atkins was one of the smartest people I had ever known when it came to the street life. Had she been born to wealthy parents she might've ended up at Princeton or Yale, but she was hood and would more likely end up in Metro State Prison for Women. The girl was a criminal if I ever saw one. She stood about five-feet-eight-inches tall and had more curves than a California freeway. And even though she was only sixteen years old, she was a seasoned pro at hustling men three times her age. It didn't hurt that she looked to be in her early twenties. She was an opportunist who never met a person she couldn't find a way to take advantage of. I never liked her, but she always seemed to be up in my face, smiling and trying to figure me out.

Shemika was the enforcer of the crew. She was big, quiet, and possessed a heart that was so cold it could freeze fire. I liked her a lot because I saw right through her tough exterior. Beneath it all was a girl who would give you the shirt off her back. She was also gay as a bird.

"Give me a second," I said and turned around and walked back into the apartment to grab my book bag. I don't know why I didn't tell them to keep driving or even why they would assume I would go with them, since I ignored them seven days a week. But there was something weird about the way the night was shaking up. I needed to get away and they were offering me what I needed.

"Where you headed with that bag, girl?" Kecia said as she popped the locks to the door. I pulled on the handle and got in behind her and threw my bags into the cargo area of the truck.

"I don't know. I can't stay with that woman anymore. She's ridiculous," I said.

"So where are you going to stay?" Kecia asked.

"Probably my grandma's house," I said. "I don't have much of a choice. Where y'all going?"

"We're going to see a man about a mule," Tiny said as she stared at her flawless MAC makeup in the lighted mirror of the passenger seat.

"Never have to worry about getting a straight answer from you," I said as I slipped my seat belt around me.

"Awww," Tiny said with a laugh. "Mrs. Goody Two-shoes buckling up."

I ignored her and turned to my backseat mate. "How you doing, Shemika?"

"I'm straight," the big girl said. "What's up with you?"

"Drama," I said. "But I'm done with that. It's time to move on."

"We're going to make a little money," Kecia said. "You down?"

"Depends," I said.

"It's all aboveboard," Kecia said. "Just gonna meet up with some guys and hang out."

"And they pay you to hang out at ten o'clock at night?" I asked.

"Listen," Tiny said, slapping the mirror closed. "You wanna go or not?"

"How about not," I snapped. "Pull over."

"Nah," Kecia said, never taking her foot off the gas pedal. "Trust me, you wanna go here."

Tiny turned around and stared at me as if she was trying to send a message that she was in charge.

"Whatchu looking at?" I barked. I never liked the girl and I was sure the feeling was mutual.

She rolled her eyes and snickered before turning back around.

"That's a smart move. Turn your butt around and stay out of my face before I fix that makeup," I said.

"Wake up," Tiny said.

"If you say one more word to me, I swear I'ma snatch that weave out of your head and beat you like you stole something."

"Chill out," Shemika said, calmly playing her role as Tiny's bodyguard. "Ain't gonna be no fighting up in here."

"Stevie Nichols is having a party," Kecia said, changing the subject. "Speak of the devil."

Kecia turned up the radio and bobbed her head to the hottest rapper alive. Stevie Nichols's voice was coming through the truck's top-notch speakers, singing the song that had the streets rocking.

*Swagged up from the floor up, Patrón got me tore up. Chasing checks and sex. I swear I need to grow up. Money's on my mind, I'm in constant grind. And my Rolly say it's Polo time.*

"He's got a lil thing for Tiny, so we going along for the ride," she said as she turned the radio down a little.

"The real Stevie Nichols? The rapper?" I asked, excited.

"Yeah, girl," she said, smiling. "The one and only. So you know the place gonna be packed with big ballers and them pockets gonna be faaaattttt."

I felt myself growing excited just at the thought of meeting the hottest rapper in America right now. His debut CD was already double platinum, and you couldn't turn on the radio or television without hearing him or seeing him.

We were on highway I-20 West for about ten minutes when we came upon Six Flags amusement park. Kecia slowed down and we got off on the Thornton Road exit. We made a right and then a quick left until we were on a dark, two-lane road. A few minutes later we came to a driveway with lights flashing, and I could hear the music from where we were. There were two guys standing by a large gate wearing headsets and fluorescent vests. They were waving little flashlights. Kecia turned into the driveway and stopped. She pushed the button to let the window down.

"Name," one of the men said as he walked up to the driver side.

"I'm Tiny. Stevie Nichols's special guest," Tiny said proudly as she leaned over Kecia.

"Tiny," the guy said, as he looked down at a clipboard that he held with one hand. "Tiny what?"

"Just Tiny," she said, then sat back in her seat.

"Yeah. You're good. Y'all look a lil young," the guy said, shining his light into the vehicle.

"Looks can be deceiving," Tiny said.

"Yeah, I'm sure," the security guy said with a stern look.

"So can we go in or not?" Kecia asked.

"Yeah," he said reluctantly. "You young ladies go on and have a good time. No alcohol."

Tiny rolled her eyes again and motioned for Kecia to drive away.

"I'm glad he didn't ask for IDs," Shemika said. "We'd be jacked up."

"No. *He* would be jacked up because I would've called Stevie and his butt would be looking for a new job," Tiny said, feeling herself a little too much.

We pulled up to a very large house. I don't even think I had seen anything like this on *MTV Cribs*. And people were everywhere.

"They shooting a video or something?" Shemika asked.

"Nah," Tiny said as if she was in the in-crowd. "It's just a party. This is how Stevie Nichols do it. This is an every-night thing. Believe that."

The long, curvy driveway was filled with luxury cars. We

parked behind a white Bentley with a young guy sitting on the hood talking on a cell phone.

We walked up about twenty steps to the front door of the mansion and walked in. We went straight through the foyer and living room, then outside to the back where there were at least four hundred people dancing in bathing suits—or less.

Stevie Nichols had to be at least twenty-eight, maybe even thirty years old, and I couldn't help but wonder why he would invite a bunch of underage girls to his party. He was standing by the pool wearing a pair of white shorts, a white tank top, some white Air Max 95s, a white hat, and some dark shades that were also trimmed in white. He was shorter than he appeared on television, but I didn't care. He was Stevie Nichols. His neck and wrists were covered with platinum jewelry, which contrasted nicely against his pecan-tan complexion. He looked our way, did a double take, then walked over and stood before us. I couldn't believe the guy who I watched on television and heard on the radio was standing right in front of me.

"Baby gurl," he said to Tiny, showing a mouthful of diamond and platinum teeth. He gave her a hug and stared me up and down over her shoulder while he held her close. "You done made my night," he said while his eyes were roaming my body.

"Nah," Tiny said. "You made my night."

"Who is this long, tall drink of water?" Stevie Nichols asked as he pulled away. "Introduce me."

"That's ole lame Jasmine. We decided to let her roll with the Divas to see how we do things," Tiny said, smiling like a Cheshire cat.

"Welcome to the party, Jasmine," he said and reached out his hand for mine.

I shook his hand and he held on to mine a little too long for my taste. I pulled back and he smiled as if to say he could have me if he wanted me. He was wrong. I wasn't interested in being one of his groupies. I already wanted to leave. There was something about older guys looking at me like I was a piece of meat that turned my stomach.

"Y'all make ya selves at home," he said, then whispered something into Tiny's ear. She nodded and smiled.

"Time to work," Tiny said, turning to us. "These dudes are drunk and most of them got plenty of cash in their pockets. Let's make sure we leave here with it in ours."

"Jasmine," she said to me, "Stevie said he has a job for you. Take it. He pays well. You don't have a place to stay, so save the stuck-up act. Get that money."

# 6

## JASMINE

I was running. I hadn't run track in three years, but all of
my training and breathing techniques came back as if I
had just left a competition meet. I wasn't sure where I was
or where I was headed, but I had to get away. All of these
men were pulling at me as if I was a piece of steak and
they were hungry lions, so I ran. Somehow I got away
from them and now I wasn't sure where I was. There was
nothing anywhere around me but trees and sticks. I
needed to rest, so I leaned against a tree to catch my
breath. I had never seen it this dark out before, but then
again, I had never been in the forest at three o'clock in the
morning. I was scared out of my mind. I listened close to
see if the men were coming. I heard something. The sticks
and leaves were crunching under the weight of something
or someone. I stood as still as I could. I held my breath because I didn't want to give whoever was out there any clue
as to my whereabouts. The crunching came closer and I
wasn't even sure if I was breathing or not. I stood perfectly

still. Then out of nowhere, a light blasted my face. I was completely blinded and I threw my hand up over my eyes. A large hand clamped down on my shoulder and another one went over my mouth. I was being dragged away, but I couldn't make a sound. I tried to get away, but whoever had me was strong as an ox and my attempts to break free were futile. I felt helpless and the more I tried to move, the harder the man's hand seemed to grip my mouth.

I jumped and looked around.

I wasn't in the woods at all. I was in a bed, and that wasn't a flashlight that was shining in my face, it was the sun. I looked around the room—it was about the same size as our entire apartment in the Bluff, but that was the last thing on my mind. I needed to find out why I was in this large room in the first place. I jumped up from the bed and ran toward the closed bedroom door. I flung it open and ran down the stairs. This was the same house that was filled with party people last night, but now it was like a ghost house.

"Hello," I said loud enough for the world to hear, but all I got in return was the echo of my own voice bouncing off the high ceilings. I walked toward the front door and snatched it open. The long, curvy driveway was empty.

"What in the heck is going on? And where is everybody?"

The last thing I remembered was coming to a party with my girls.

I left the door open and walked back into the house. I needed to get to my phone, but remembered I left it at home. I walked into the kitchen and looked around, but didn't see one. I saw my book bag sitting on the island in the middle of the kitchen and my duffel bag was on the floor beside it. They seemed to have been untouched. There was a mirror on the wall outside in the hallway. I ran over to it and looked at myself. Nothing seemed out of order. My clothes seemed undisturbed. I sighed and scratched my head. Where was everybody? I walked around the house not knowing what to think.

"Hi," a male voice said from above me.

"I need to go home," I said as I looked up to the second floor of the large house at a man whom I had never seen before.

He smiled. "Sure. Are you okay?"

"I'm fine," I said. "I just need to go home."

"I'll be right down," he said and walked down the stairs toward me. I was nervous, but I didn't show it. He seemed to be in his early twenties and had a nice build, as if he worked out on a regular basis. And he was fine. I couldn't help but realize that and he had a swagger that said he was happy in his own skin.

"Did you have a good time last night?" he said as he walked over to a desk that sat in the corner of the open living room and opened the drawer.

"I don't even remember much about last night. Why was I in a bed? Did somebody rape me?" I asked as my voice cracked.

The guy shook his chocolate face and sighed. "No. No one touched you. I put you in my room and I made sure nobody came near you."

"You put me there? Why did you do that?"

"Yes, I put you there—and why? Well, let's just say I thought you'd be more comfortable there versus sleeping on the kitchen floor, which was where you were sprawled out," he said. He sat down at the desk. After fiddling around inside the open drawer, he found what he was looking for and closed the drawer.

"Why was I on the kitchen floor?"

"I rent my house out for video shoots and parties from time to time. Those rapper guys are animals and I really don't like dealing with them, but they seem to like to throw money away so I take it. Anyway, you seemed really nice and didn't appear to want any part of their foolishness, so I took it upon myself to keep you away from them."

"I don't remember anything except coming to the party and meeting Stevie Nichols."

"Yes, you were at a party and yes, Stevie Nichols was here. And I'm sure one of his friends slipped something into your drink. Anyway, you were taken care of. I had a friend of mine put you in my room. I slept upstairs in the guest room."

"And those girls that I was with, where are they?"

"I don't know. I'm not sure who you came with."

He pulled out his iPhone and started flipping around the screen. He held up a finger to me and spoke to someone on the phone. "Hi there. This is Barry Dasher. I need a car to come out and get a friend of mine to . . ." He looked at me for my destination.

"The Bluff. It's over off of Joseph E. Boone Boulevard. Not too far from Clark Atlanta University."

He repeated what I said, thanked the person he was talking to, and then he hung up the phone.

"I called a car service for you and they should be here shortly. I have a lot of work to do or I would take you myself," he said with one of the most pleasant smiles I had ever seen.

"That's cool."

"I'm Barry," he said, standing and walking over to where I was standing. He extended his hand to me. "Barry Dasher."

I shook his hand and looked around the house again. It was straight out of a magazine.

"What time is it?"

"A little after one."

"You live here with your family?"

"Nope," Barry said. "It's just me."

"Why do you have this big ole house just for you?"

"I like it, and it's really not as big as it seems."

"What do you do for a living to have a place like this? You look young," I asked. I knew I was being a little nosy, but what did I have to lose?

"I do a few different things. I'm a stockbroker and I'm a photographer. Guess which one pays the bills?" he said with that smile again.

"The stocks," I said.

"Yes, but photography makes me happy. So hopefully one day it'll pay the bills."

"I hope you get what you want, but if I lived in a place like this, I would keep on doing what I'm doing."

"How old are you? I never got your name."

"I turned sixteen today and my name is Jasmine."

"Well, happy birthday, Jasmine," Barry said, then walked over to a wall cabinet and came out with an expensive-looking camera. "Do you mind if I take a few snapshots of ya?"

"Ahh, yeah," I said, covering my face. "I look a mess."

Barry smiled and snapped a picture anyway.

"Man," I said, "don't do that."

"Okay," he said. "But while you wait on your ride, would you like to see some of my work?"

"Yeah, that's cool," I said. "Just don't take no pictures of me."

"Okay." He motioned for me to come over and sit with him on a white leather sofa. It was almost too pretty to sit on, but he just plopped down on it and grabbed a photo album from the stainless steel coffee table.

"These are all celebrities," he said.

"Are you one of these paparazzi kind of dudes that work for TMZ?"

"Nah," he said. "I actually get permission to take my shots."

"You didn't get permission from me," I said.

"True," he said with a smile and flipped open his book.

Inside were pictures of everybody who was anybody. He had Jermaine Dupri and Janet Jackson, Simon and Fantasia from *American Idol*, Trey Songz, Chris Brown, Jay-Z, Willow Smith, Diggy Simmons, and lots of other people who were big shots in their fields.

The doorbell rang and Barry handed me the book and stood up. "Your ride is here," he said.

He opened the door and a white guy wearing a black suit and what looked like an old train conductor's hat stood there with a big smile on his face.

"How are ya?" Barry said. "Come on in. Her bags are over there in the kitchen."

The driver handed him a slip of paper and he signed it and gave it back to him. The driver walked over and picked up both of my bags, then walked back outside.

"Well, Miss Jasmine," Barry said, "I hope everything

goes well in your life. My suggestion is for you to get into modeling. You are a natural."

"Yeah, right. I was always called the ugly duckling."

"Yet now you're a beautiful swan," he said. "If you ever want to get a portfolio together, give me a call. I like to think I know beauty, and you have what it takes."

"Me? Prancing around on *America's Next Top Model*?" I said with a frown. "Nah. I can't even imagine that."

"Take my card. Think about it. What do you have to lose?"

"Thanks for looking out for me last night," I said as I stood by the door. "Most guys wouldn't do that."

"Do I look like most guys?"

I looked around the opulent house and then back at him.

"Nah," I said as I took his business card. "You're far from most guys. Thanks again."

"Don't mention it," Barry said and waved good-bye.

I walked down the steps of the mansion and out to a black Lincoln Town Car where the driver was standing by the open back door. He waited for me to get inside and closed the door behind me. I looked out the window at the big house and couldn't help but wonder if I really had what it took to be a model, or if that guy was just running game. I decided to find out. We had just pulled onto the long driveway leading us away from the big house when I asked the driver to stop the car. I reached in my pocket and pulled out the business card that Barry had just given me.

"May I use your phone?" I asked the driver.

"There is one back there. Lift the armrest," he said.

I did and there was the phone. I picked it up and dialed

the cell phone number on the card. He answered on the second ring.

"Hi, this is Jasmine. I just left your house."

"What's up?"

"I need a place to stay. Can you help me?"

"Have the driver bring you back."

"Okay," I said, feeling my heart pick up its pace.

"We'll figure something out."

I nodded and hung up the phone. "Turn around, please. I'm going back to the house."

# 7

## DeMarco

Dave & Buster's was packed with people who seemed to be doing well in life. Some of them seemed outright rich. I felt like a fish out of water. I was self-conscious and paranoid. I don't know why, but I had the feeling that everyone was looking at me and Devin. I gripped his little hand as he tried to run off to a big playpen filled with colorful balls.

"I wanna get in that," he said with big bright eyes.

"Okay," I said as I let his hand go, but picked up my pace to keep him in my sight.

I had never seen so many white people in my life and to be honest, they made me nervous.

Devin ran up the ladder, and a white girl with blond hair that was pulled back into a ponytail, piercing blue eyes, and a Dave & Buster's sun visor on her head, stopped him in his tracks.

"No shoes, buddy," she said with a stern face.

Devin frowned and backed up. He dropped his head and turned around and started crying.

I was ready to pounce on her, but I remained calm. I reached out to pick up Devin, but the white girl came running over with her hand over her mouth as if she would again let something foul slip out.

"Noooo," the white girl said, reaching out to grab Devin's arm. "I'm sorry."

I started to snap on her, but since she apologized I remained silent.

"Today is my birthday," Devin said, pointing at the ten-foot-high net cage with the colorful balls and twenty-or-so kids playing. "I wanna play in the balls."

"You can play, buddy. You just have to take off your shoes," she said with genuine concern on her face.

Devin wiped his eyes and looked up at me as if to ask if he should trust the girl.

"Go ahead and take your shoes off," I said.

I was happy that we went to Foot Locker and got new shoes and socks before we came here. I would've been super embarrassed if he removed his shoes and showed those dirty socks that were filled with holes. I tossed those in the trash and paid ten dollars for a new six-pack. I also got Devin a pair of Air Max 95s just like the ones I bought for myself.

"Okay," he said, wiping the remainder of his tears away.

"And guess what else," the white girl said. "Since it's your birthday and I made a big goof, I'm going to make it up to you with a birthday surprise. Will that be okay?"

That got him to smile and his eyes lit up.

"You can get in, too," the white girl said to me. "It's a lot of fun."

"Oh no. I'm good," I said.

"I love that tattoo," she said. "Is that some kind of tribal mark?"

"Yes," I said, even though it wasn't.

"I love it," she said.

"Thanks," I said.

"You must be his big brother," she said.

"Yeah," I said. "Just getting him out to have some fun for his birthday."

"How old is he?"

"Three."

"Cool," she said. "I'm going to get him some cake and ice cream if that's okay with you."

"That's cool," I said.

"And I'll see if I can't find some candles. I really didn't mean to make him cry."

"No big deal," I said to the extrafriendly white girl.

"Be right back," she said.

I waved my hand at her and walked over to the large mesh ball thingy to watch Devin. He made his way over to some white kids who looked to be a few years older than him. He handed one of the kids a ball as a form of introduction. The little white kid took it and thanked him. I watched as my little brother bounced around with the other kids, having the time of his life. I loved every minute of it. Somehow he made it over to where I was standing and smiled.

"You having a good time, dude?"

"Yeah," he said, overwhelmed with excitement. He pointed at a little white kid and an Asian boy. "Those are my friends."

"Cool."

"Can I ride the motorcycle?"

"Fa'sho," I said. "Come on out and let's get you back in your shoes."

Devin nodded his head and slowly but surely made his way to the entrance.

"I'm going to the motorcycles. Bye," he said to his new friends.

"Bye, Devin," the guys said.

I met Devin by the entrance and lifted him up and sat him down on the bench. I placed his shoes back on his little feet and held his hand as we walked over to the games.

"Hey," Blondie, the white girl, said. "Are you guys eating here?"

"Yeah," I said. "If I can get him to take a break from the games."

"He seems to be having a ball. I feel so bad that I made him cry."

"Don't sweat it," I said.

"I have him an ice cream cake and a special gift. Soooo, I'll find you guys when you eat and bring them over. We'll have the crew sing 'Happy Birthday' to him as well."

"That's real nice of you," I said.

"Bye, Devin," she said with a bubbly smile.

"Bye," he said, waving his little hand. "Can we get on the motorcycles now?"

"I'm following you," I said and watched my little brother as he took off running toward the games.

After about an hour of games, we sat down for dinner. True to her word, the bubbly white girl came over with an ice cream cake and about ten more people in tow. They started clapping and singing "Happy Birthday."

Devin was so excited he couldn't contain himself. The

white girl came over and handed him a big balloon and a shiny blue bag with a bunch of tissue paper in it.

"Happy birthday, Devin," she said.

Devin's eyes grew bigger than they had been all night, and he tore through the paper and pulled out a big red car with DAVE & BUSTER'S on the doors and hood.

"Thank you," he said, and got out of his seat and gave the girl a hug.

"Oh my God," the girl said as if she was about to cry. "You are so sweet."

Once the cake was eaten, Devin and I said our good-byes to the extrafriendly people of Dave & Buster's. It was dark outside. I looked at the clock on my cell phone. We had arrived at the mall at four thirty and now it was after nine o'clock at night.

We made our way to the main street in front of Cumberland Mall and waited at the MARTA bus stop.

"Did you have a good time, lil bro?"

"Yeah," he said with that wide smile. "Can we come again?"

"Fa'sho," I said.

The bus pulled up and we got on. Devin sat beside me looking out the window at all the roaring cars. He couldn't keep quiet as he had something to say about every car or big building he saw. I was lost in my own world, wondering why I was born poor and why these people were born into a life of surplus. Did God really like my kind? As we rode, I thought back to our day. We had a good time. We bought new clothes and shoes, and had celebrated our birthdays with some of the nicest people I had ever met, and ninety percent of them were white. The only time I ever saw white people was when I was getting locked up or being sentenced in one of their courts. I thought I didn't like white folks, but I had to admit, we had a good time. I wanted more of this life. A slight gloom took over me as I thought about what was waiting on us once we left the clean streets of Smyrna and hit the dirtiness of the Bluff. I looked down at my little brother and he had laid his head on my arm and was fast asleep. The bus rumbled a little more, then came to a stop at the train station. I lifted Devin, grabbed our bags, and jumped off the bus and onto a train. Thirty minutes later, we were on another bus that would take us to the Bluff. The driver nodded to me and gave me a thumbs-up. The bus was packed and I dreaded standing the entire ride while holding a forty-pound little boy. A guy about my age tapped me on the leg and nodded that I could have his seat.

"Lil man knocked out, huh?" the guy said.

"Yeah," I said as we sat down. "Long day."

"DeMarco," a velvety voice said from beside me.

I turned to see who was calling my name and my eyes came across the prettiest girl in the world. Morgan Hughes was my childhood girlfriend. She was my girl-friend in third grade and I'd been trying to get her to give me the time of day ever since, but she wasn't trying to hear me. Most folks thought she was into girls because she dressed like a tomboy, but I knew the real Morgan. She had the smoothest chocolate skin I had ever seen. She was only four-feet-nine-inches tall, but she stood out like a giant to me. She played on the school's basketball team as a point guard, ran the 100- and 400-meter relays on the track team, and was in all kinds of academic clubs. She was one of the, if not *the*, most popular girls at James Charles High School. She always wore her hair in those tiny microbraids and dressed like one of the boys. I looked at her gear and she was wearing a pair of baggy basketball shorts, a tank top, and some three-quarter-length Jordans.

"Hey, girl," I said, smiling from ear to ear. "What's good wit cha?"

"Where have you been, boy?" she said with a frown.

"Locked up," I said.

"Dag," she said, shaking her head. "And you say it with so much pride. 'Locked up,'" she mocked with her chest stuck out. "That's something to whisper and mumble, not sing for the world to hear."

"Nah, I feel ya," I said. "Just telling you the truth."

"You are so much more than that, Dee," she said and looked at me with pity. I didn't like that look.

I nodded my head in response.

"This is my stop. Are you coming back to Charles?"

"Yeah," I said. "I'll be there early in the morning."

"That's what's up," Morgan said as she stood. She reached out and rubbed Devin's head and then ran her soft hand across my face. "Bye, Dee. I hope I see you at school tomorrow. Find me tomorrow, okay?"

"Fa'sho," I said.

There was something about the way she looked at me that told me she wanted to see more of me. I had seen that look before, but I couldn't seem to stay out of jail long enough for us to really get reacquainted with each other. Her touch sent chills down my spine. It was a feeling that I had never felt before. I wanted more of it. I was sixteen and, in the hood, that was old. It was especially old to still be a virgin. Guys my age had been having sex for years, but being that I stayed locked up so much, I never really had the opportunity. I was still a virgin, but that one touch got me to thinking I was ready for bigger and better things. But I knew Morgan wasn't the kind of girl to just get with any ole body. So I had to make sure that I wasn't going to be any ole body.

# 8

## DeMarco

We got off the bus and walked across the busy Joseph E. Lowery Boulevard. It was almost ten o'clock at night now, and people were still out as if it was the middle of the day. I was happy to see my hood because Devin was getting heavier and heavier by the second. My arms felt like they were going to fall off as sharp pains shot through my shoulder blades from holding him. All I could think about was getting home and putting his butt down. Just as I made it to the sidewalk and turned onto my street, I saw something that forced me to pause. Was that what I thought it was? Up under the lone streetlight at the end of the street was the last thing I wanted to see. My heart began to race and all of a sudden I wasn't concerned about my aching arms anymore. I stared down my block and noticed about four or five white police cruisers idling in front of our apartment. I was conflicted about continuing on my way. I had just gotten home and wasn't ready to go back to jail. As I walked in slow motion toward my house, my thoughts were interrupted by my new white neighbor.

Mrs. Eichelberger was sitting on a swing on her front porch, and when she saw me she stood up and called out to me. I stopped but kept my eyes on my house.

"DeMarco," she said, and there was something in her voice now that wasn't there earlier. I sensed fear when I turned to look at her; I saw the same fear in her eyes.

"Yes," I said calmly, but my mind was racing in over-drive. I knew those cars weren't there for the old people who lived across from us or the middle-aged Bible-thumper who lived directly above them. I wasn't sure, but more than likely they weren't there for the Muslim couple who lived above us. No, in my history when cops came to our location, they were there for me. One hundred per-cent of the time—but what did I do? I hadn't been home long enough to do anything. My brain searched for a rea-son for them to be there. Why would they send so many cars for just little old me? Did someone frame me? That wasn't out of the question. The hood was filled with snitches who weren't above pointing the finger at who-ever they thought could help get the heat off of them. Did Mr. P break the law by signing me out, and were those clowns there to take me back to my cell at Metro? A mil-lion and one questions attacked my brain.

"There was a shooting down there," Mrs. Eichelberger said. "At your place."

"A shooting? At my place?" I asked. "Who was shooting who?"

"I don't know," she said. "But the police have been down there for about an hour. They also came around here asking about Devin."

"What?" I said as I started walking toward the house.

"DeMarco," she said in a soothing yet desperate voice. "I know you don't know me, but I'm very trustworthy. Will you leave Devin here with me while you go and check on your house? I promise you I won't harm him."

"Why would I do that?" I asked.

"I think they want to take him," she said. "The police officer said he needed to get him over to the Department of Family and Children Services. I will take care of him. I don't want to see him in foster care. My husband and I are here alone. We can help for as long as you need us to. Please allow us to do that."

She could've saved the plea. Once she said *foster care*, I knew taking Devin down to the house wasn't an option.

"Yeah," I said as I walked back to her gate. She opened it for me and I dropped my bags and used both my hands to pass Devin to her. My little brother never woke up. He just adjusted his arms from around my neck to Mrs. Eichelberger's. He wrapped his legs around her waist and laid his head on her shoulder. "I will be back in a few."

"Okay," she said and quickly turned and made her way into her house.

I took a deep breath, stretched out my arms, picked up my bags, and headed down the street to see what kind of foolishness awaited me.

When I walked up to our apartment, a young black police officer, who appeared to be a rookie, met me and stopped me from going into the house.

"And you are?" he asked, pulling out a small notepad.

"I'm DeMarco. I live here."

"How old are you?"

"What's going on?" I asked, ignoring the man's inquiry. "Where is my sister?"

"What is your sister's name?"

"Jasmine."

"How old is she?"

"Why do you keep asking me how old somebody is, man? Where is my sister?"

"Calm down."

"I'm calm. I asked you, where is my sister?"

"What is your mother's name?"

"Sophia," I said. "Now you wanna tell me where my sister is?"

"I don't know where your sister is, but your mother is right there."

I turned and looked just in time to see my mother being led out of the house in handcuffs.

"What the . . . ," I said to myself and walked over to her. The rookie didn't try to stop me.

"She was right," Sophia said, shaking her head. "My daughter was right."

"What's going on?" I asked.

"I killed him. I killed him dead. That's right, I did it. I shot him right in his dumb head and I'm proud of it."

"Stop talking like that, Sophia. Don't say nothing else," I said to my mother. She looked like she had consumed an entire fifth of gin. She paid me no attention and continued ranting and raving about her shooting somebody as she was being led to a waiting police car with her hands cuffed behind her back.

"Son," a different officer said to me. The guy was tall and heavyset and I couldn't tell if he was black or white. "Is that your mother?"

"Yes," I said. "What is she talking about?"

"Do you live here with her?"

"Yes."

"How old are you?"

"I'm sixteen," I said.

"Do you have any relative that you can stay with?"

"My grandmother," I said.

"Does she live around here?"

"Not too far," I said.

"The house is now a crime scene and I suggest you go to your grandmother's house or we'll have to take you to DFCS."

"I'm good," I said. "I'll go to my grandma's house in a few. What's going on here?"

"Your little brother, Devin," he said, reading from a notepad. "Where is he? Is he at your grandmother's house?"

"He's fine. He's in good hands," I said. "Now will you please tell me what's up?"

"We need to confirm that your brother is with a relative," the officer said.

"Yes," I lied. "He's with a relative. Do you need for me to take you to see him?"

"No. I just needed to know that he was with a family member," the officer said as if he was just going through the motions of another murder investigation in the hood.

"I need to talk to my mom before y'all take her away. Can I do that?"

"Let me check," he said. "Here is my card. If you would like to talk to me about anything, please don't hesitate to call me. I will keep you abreast of what's going on with your mother. Do you have a number where I can get in touch with you?"

I shook my head and took the card and stuck it in my back pocket.

"I'll speak with my supervisor and get right back to you. Stay right here for now," the cop said.

I never liked nor did I trust the police, yet this guy was standing here acting like he was Officer Friendly.

I stood in place for about two or three minutes. A different police officer walked by. He looked familiar. The more I stared at him, the more I realized who he was. He was the last officer to arrest me. Now here he was taking my mother away in what was probably the same car that took me away the last time.

"Yo," I called out to the officer. "What is my mom talking about? Who did she say she killed?"

The officer just looked at me and kept walking. I walked over to a young white officer who was standing in front of my apartment. I wasn't really worried. I heard my mom say she killed *him*. As long as Jasmine was okay, I was good. But since my mom was in the middle of some crap, I wanted to know what was going on. Death, police, arrest, and jail had been such a constant in my life that I wasn't even feeling anything. Seeing my mother being led away in handcuffs didn't affect me one way or the other, and that bothered me. I stood there on the sidewalk staring at the chaos that was swarming around me like flies on a corpse, and didn't even flinch.

"Apparently, your mother shot her boyfriend. She said she caught him looking at her daughter in the shower," the cop said.

"Where is my sister?"

The cop ignored me and kept walking. I walked up to another officer and asked him.

"Where is my sister?"

"Who is your sister?"

I knew better than to give the police any more information than was absolutely necessary, so I just said: "She lives here."

"Oh. Nobody is here but your mother and her boyfriend. Well, technically he's not here anymore."

"What happened?" I asked.

"Your mother said the boyfriend was video recording the daughter while she was in the shower. Seems to me that Momma didn't like that, so she put an end to it. A bullet in the head is a good way to go about it," the officer said nonchalantly.

I stood there and sighed. The first officer that I was speaking to called me over. I walked over to where he was standing.

"I'm going to give you two minutes to speak with your mother," he said, then sat in the driver's seat and let the backseat window down about two inches. He got out of the car and darted off toward the apartment, which was now the latest crime scene in a long line of crime scenes in the Bluff.

I tapped on the window and my mother stopped rocking and looked at me.

"It's a good thing I got that hug from you today," she

said with a smile. "Ain't no telling when I'll be able to touch you again."

"What happened?"

"I don't want to talk about it. Let's just say, I was wrong for not listening to Jaz. She was right about that old no-good fool."

"Where is Jasmine?"

"I don't know," she said, dropping her head in shame.

"Well, Devin is good. He's down the street with that white lady. The one who lives in that house with the gate."

She nodded her head. "Mrs. Eichelberger is a good woman. Let him stay there. She'll take good care of him. You and Jaz old enough now to take care of yourselves. I'll be a'ight."

"Who is this guy you shot?"

"Otis," she said in disgust. "What the hell he wants with a chile when he got a grown woman right in his face?"

I looked at my mother. Her skin was covered with dark spots. She looked like she was at least fifty-five years old, yet she was only thirty-one. She had never been to jail in her life, but she was calm, as if this were a daily routine.

I reached my hand through the little slit in the window and she leaned her head over for me to touch her.

"I'll come check on you tomorrow."

"Don't worry 'bout me," she said. "I'll be fine. Go find your sister and tell her I said stay wherever she is and don't worry 'bout me either."

"A'ight," I said.

The police officer walked up and got in the driver seat.

"Okay," he said. "I gotta take her."

I stepped back and stared at my mother. Sophia leaned back in the seat and turned away from me. She seemed tired, defeated, and jail was a welcome relief from the hard-edged life of the Bluff. Unfortunately I knew the feeling all too well.

# 9

# DeMarco

Once all but one of the police left, I was allowed inside our apartment to gather a few of my things. They were still treating the place as a crime scene so I had to hurry. I didn't have much that I needed, since I hadn't been home in so long. I grabbed my toothbrush, deodorant, and a few pair of underwear, and walked out. The police officer who was standing by the door locked up behind me and asked me if I needed a ride to my grandmother's house. I thanked him but said no thanks.

I needed to find Jasmine. I threw my book bag over my shoulder and walked down the street to Mrs. Eichelberger's house. I let myself into the gate and walked down the stone pathway until I came to her porch. A light was on in the front room and I could see a television's blue light dance off of the walls. I walked up the stairs and rang the doorbell.

"Who is it?" a male voice said from the other side of the door.

"DeMarco from down the street," I said.

I heard a few locks disengage and the door swung open. A tall white man with long hair pulled back into a ponytail stood before me with a smile on his face. He had a clean-shaven face and had two hoop earrings in each of his earlobes.

"How are ya?" the man said.

"I'm good," I said. "I need to pick up my little brother."

"Yeah, sure. Come on in," he said and backed away from the door to allow me room. "I'm Scott; Michelle's husband. How are you?"

I walked into the house and my skin welcomed the coolness of the air conditioner. The house was as awesome on the inside as it was on the outside. It didn't look like anything I had ever seen in the Bluff. They had hardwood floors and a stone fireplace with a large flat-screen television hanging above it. They had white shelves with books for days. Devin was lying on a leather sofa beside Mrs. Eichelberger, who was sitting with a laptop on her thighs. She had on a pair of wire-rimmed glasses and looked like a schoolteacher. She removed her glasses and placed them and the computer on the table beside her. She stood when I walked in.

"Is everything okay?" Mrs. Eichelberger asked.

"No," I said, shaking my head. "The police took my mom. I think she shot her boyfriend."

"Did he die?" Scott Eichelberger asked with a look of genuine concern on his face.

"I don't know. I think so," I said.

"I'm sorry to hear that," he said. "Can we offer you something to drink?"

"No," I said. "I just need to grab Devin so we can get out of y'all hair."

"Where are you guys going?" she asked.

"To my grandmother's house. It's not too far from here."

"DeMarco," Mrs. Eichelberger said, shooting a look to her husband, "I know you don't know us very well, but we want to help. We would love to watch Devin for you until you get yourself settled," the woman said.

I contemplated her offer. My mom did say to leave Devin with her, but to me that was kind of rude to just pawn your kid off on some white folks. But then again, I needed to find Jasmine and get myself together. Grandma wasn't in any kind of shape to be running after Devin, and Uncle Moochie wasn't responsible enough to watch a goldfish, nevermind a child.

"For how long?" I asked.

"For as long as you need us to," Scott Eichelberger said.

"Okay," I said. "I can leave you guys a few bucks."

"No," Mrs. Eichelberger said. "Save your money. He's fine."

"Well," I said, not sure what to say. "I will come by and check on him tomorrow. Hopefully I can get settled in at my grandmother's in a few days and I'll come back to get him."

"Take your time," Scott said. "You have a lot going on. Devin is fine. We'll treat him like royalty."

I sighed. Something didn't feel right about leaving my brother with a bunch of strangers. White strangers at that! I would feel much better leaving him with Mrs. Gloria or somebody. I had a feeling that Devin was in good hands, but I still didn't feel right leaving him.

"Okay," I said. I walked over and stood over my sleeping little brother. He'd had a long day and seemed to be sleeping so peacefully. I didn't want to wake him, so I just reached out and touched his little head. "He needs a haircut. I will come over tomorrow after school and take him to get one."

"Take him with you too," Mrs. Eichelberger said, pointing at her husband.

"Hey," Scott said. "What are you talking about? No barber in his right mind would cut this."

I chuckled and reached down to pick up my bags.

Scott and his wife walked over to me. They looked at each other, then Scott spoke up. "You know you're more than welcome to stay too."

"I'm good," I said, wondering what kind of people I was dealing with. I understood them taking Devin in—he was just a little kid—but I was bigger than both of them, fresh out of juvey, and saw the way they had looked at me when I walked in. Their eyes registered fear, but obviously something inside of them was overruling that feeling. "Thanks for the offer, but y'all already doing enough."

"Okay," Mrs. Eichelberger said, and I could've sworn I saw relief on her face.

"I'll be back tomorrow to take Devin to get a haircut, and if I'm settled, I'll take him off your hands. Can I have a phone number where I can reach y'all? I'll give you mine too."

"Sure, and no rush. We love having Devin over," Mrs. Eichelberger said, then walked over to her end table and scribbled their number on a Post-it note. She handed me the number, then rubbed my arm in a reassuring kind of way. "You take care of yourself out there, DeMarco, and call us if you need us."

Scott Eichelberger reached out and shook my hand. He had a flimsy and weak grip, but he smiled and used his free hand to pat my shoulder as if we were old friends.

I walked out of the Eichelbergers' home not knowing which way to turn. Once I was out of the gate on the sidewalk, I turned around and looked back at the nice home in the middle of the hood. *Devin is living it up,* I thought.

I walked back down the street to our apartment and noticed that all the police were gone. It was as if nothing even happened. I needed to find my sister, so I walked past my house until I got to the end of the street. I couldn't remember which house Kecia lived in, but I knew it was at the end of the block. It was almost midnight, but folks were out like it was the middle of the day.

"Brah," I asked this guy who appeared to be about eleven years old. He was standing on the corner looking for customers for his illegal narcotics sales. "Which one of these houses does Kecia live in?"

"Who you?" he asked while scowling at me with the typical Bluff mean mug. He was already hardened and there was no fear on his bony black face.

"DeMarco, man," I said, not really in the mood to play this game tonight.

"Ohh," the boy said as if he really knew me. "When you get home?"

"Today," I said. I didn't know him, but I was pretty well-known throughout the area for my criminal exploits, my skills on the basketball court, and for my tattoos. "I'm looking for my sister. Have you seen her?"

"Nah, but Kecia lives right there. She probably know

where she at," he said and pointed to this house that was at the end of the dead-end street. There were no street-lights on because the kids got a kick out of shooting them out. As fast as the city would come and put them up, shots would ring out even faster. Finally the city said forget it and left the residents in the dark. I walked down to the end of the street and caught a break. Kecia was sitting on the front porch listening to an iPod. She was wearing a T-shirt and some pink booty shorts. I figured she was out trying to escape the heat.

"What's up, Kecia," I said as I walked up her driveway.

She pulled the plugs out of her ears and stared at me. She frowned as if she had no idea who I was.

"Have you seen my sister?" I asked. "This is Dee."

"Ohh, snap. What's up, boy," she said. "Man, you done got tall. What they feeding you in that jail?"

"Nuttin' good," I said. "Have you seen Jasmine?"

"Nah," she said. "We hung out last night, but I haven't seen her since."

"Where did y'all hang out?"

"Stevie Nichols had a party. It was off the chain. I guess she had a better time than we did because when it was time to leave, she was nowhere to be found. But some-body said they saw her on the bus today."

"So y'all just left her at the party with some rappers?"

"She was straight," Kecia said. "Jasmine can take care of herself."

"Yeah, and it's a good thing because y'all sure wasn't looking out."

"Whatever, man. That was all part of the plan. I wouldn't leave her out there like that, but if you see her tell her we

need to holla at her. She should have something that we
need to split four ways."

"Whatchu mean she got something that y'all need to
split four ways? What does she have?"

"Now you dipping ya nose where it don't belong,"
Kecia said as if I was going along with her game. Six
months ago, I would have been down with her program
and could see myself trying to get in where I fit in on their
little hustle, but I didn't want any part of that life anymore.

"Well," I said, "it was good seeing you. If you see my sister before I do, tell her to get with me ASAP. We have a family emergency."

"I will," she said. "You looking good, Dee."

"Thanks," I said.

I didn't know what Jasmine and her so-called Diva
friends had going on, but something didn't seem right. I
decided to not press the issue with Kecia since I had seen
my sister earlier in the day.

"A'ight, Kecia. Do you have a cell number for Jaz or anything?"

"Yeah," she said and flipped through her phone. I
pulled out my own phone and punched in the numbers
that she gave me.

"A'ight," I said. "Thanks a lot. I'll see you around."

"You straight," Kecia said and popped her earplugs
back into her ears and continued listening to whatever she
was enjoying before I showed up.

"Yo, Dee," the young street dealer who I spoke to earlier called out to me. "I need to get me one of those tats,
brah. I got some chetta."

"Just come holla at me tomorrow after school," I said.

"School?" he said, then pulled up two fistfuls of money. "I bet you can't get this in school."

I laughed and shook my head. "You better put that up. You'll need it for a lawyer pretty soon."

"Stop putting the jinx on me," the youngster said. "I'm smarter than you, brah brah. Po po can't touch me. I'm the new Teflon kid round here. They call me the ghost, because whenever they here, I disappear. Poof."

"I bet you are," I said as I made my way back down the street toward my apartment.

I really didn't feel like walking the two miles to my grandma's house and it was too late to go over to Jolly's. The cops said I needed to stay out of my apartment, but since when did I ever care about what they said? Never! And I wasn't about to start now.

I walked up to my front door and turned the knob; it was locked and I didn't have a key. I walked around to the back and tried the window; it was open, so I crawled through it and got inside. I flipped on the light switch and watched as what appeared to be a few hundred roaches scattered in every direction. I picked up the can of Raid that I had bought earlier and started blasting them into the roach afterlife. As I was spraying away, I looked on the hallway floor and saw splatters of blood. My eyes followed the crimson line from the floor all the way up to a big round spot on the hallway wall.

"Man," I said to myself as I held the can of bug spray in my hand, staring at the bloody wall. "Homeboy got fired up. I guess he won't be peeping at nobody else. Freak."

I went into the bathroom and sprayed some more roaches. I relieved myself, washed my hands, and decided it was time for a hot shower. I wasn't concerned about messing up the police officers' so-called crime scene. I doubted that they would even come back. Shootings, murders, robberies, rapes, and any other crime you could think of was a daily occurrence in the Bluff, and to most of the police officers who worked the area, we were all expendable.

I pulled the shower curtain back and looked down at the dirty bathtub. It had a dark ring around it that revealed it hadn't been cleaned in weeks, which was perhaps the last time Jasmine had stayed home. There was a pile of dirty clothes in it, so I pulled out the mildew-stained clothes and tossed them on the floor. I turned the faucet on to as hot as it would go and jumped in. The water felt good on my skin and I could almost feel the smell of the juvey center coming off me. I found a wrinkled-up slab of soap and lathered up every inch of my body, then stepped under the showerhead and allowed the water to completely rinse away the bubbles. After about thirty full minutes in the shower, I turned off the faucet and stepped out onto the floor. I looked around for a towel but couldn't find one. I walked out of the bathroom, crossed the living room, and walked into Jaz's room. She kept her own personal stash of towels. I opened up the closet and there they were, folded neatly in the top of her closet. I grabbed one and dried myself off. I wrapped the towel around my waist and walked into the living room. I dug around my bag for a pair of boxer underwear and a T-shirt. Once I was dressed, I plopped down on the sofa.

I was tired but still a little overwhelmed with today's events. I grabbed the remote control for the television and channel surfed until I found something that looked interesting. The apartment had an odor that wasn't the same as the one I had smelled earlier, but I guess death smelled different than anything else. I sat back, threw my feet up on the other end of the sofa, and closed my eyes. My mind raced over where I was when I woke up this morning to where I was laying my head tonight. I couldn't do anything but shake my head.

*What a birthday*, I thought as I drifted off to sleep.

# 10

# JASMINE

Nya Styles was an upscale beauty salon that sat in the heart of Buckhead. I loved Buckhead and everything that it represented. Wealth, fame, and class were all I could think about as I sat in the stylist chair. I felt like Rihanna or somebody. I felt special sitting in this high-back swivel chair. I looked out of the window of the salon and watched as one luxury vehicle after another passed by. Two different people worked on my hair and nails at the same time. Before this, the only time I had gotten my hair done was when Kecia put in my microbraids right before the basketball season. I cringed at the thought of how she would pull my hair so tight that my eyes would water. But this was different. Everything about this felt good. I had just gotten a wash, and after sitting under the blow-dryer I was now getting something else done. The guy doing my hair now was a total professional. He barely spoke, yet he was cordial. I was so used to going with Kecia to her mom's shop and hearing all of the loud gossip that was going around the hood about who was with who or this person got locked up for shooting so-and-so. Nope, no such talk went on at Nya's. The television show *The View* was on the flat screen and soft music played in the background. I had to pinch myself to make sure I wasn't dreaming. The nail technician was wiping away my old look and replacing it with a plain, clear polish topped off with some white tips. I think she called it French-something. I thought it was kind of plain, but since I wasn't paying, I wasn't complaining.

"So seems like Barry has high hopes for you," the nail lady said.

"I'm not sure what his plans are," I said. "He asked me to come here and get my hair and nails done so he could take some pictures."

"You are very pretty," the gay white guy who was doing my hair said. Finally speaking up.

"Thanks," I said. I wasn't used to hearing that. I was always called names like ugly, tall and skinny, bag of bones, and any other negative thing you call someone to hurt their feelings. Yet these white folks were standing here calling me names that made me feel good inside.

"You have great features. The camera is going to love you," the white guy said with a smile on his face.

I didn't respond. I was a fish out of water with these rich people, and I felt the less I said, the better I would be.

"All done," he said and spun my chair around for me to see what he had done.

I stared at myself and wasn't sure what to think. My hair looked pretty plain. It felt good, but it just looked like a simple bob to me—but whatever. I nodded my head.

"You like?" the guy asked me as he removed my cape.

"Yeah," I said.

"Great. Tell Barry he will have to send me some pictures so I can put them in my portfolio. I have a good feeling about you."

"Thanks," I said as I stood. "I guess I need to call him to
come pick me up."

"Your car is here," he said. "I'll call for him to come
around."

*My car? What car?* I wondered but kept my thoughts to
myself. The guy picked up the phone and said, "The
princess is ready," then hung up. *Princess? Maybe I was
dreaming.*

I had to wonder if God was playing some cruel trick on
me. Two days ago, I was sitting in one of the poorest parts
of Atlanta, scraping for food and wondering if I was going
to be molested in my sleep by some creep. My cell phone
rang and a number that I didn't recognize showed up on
the screen. Being that I didn't know the caller, I ignored it.
Different numbers had been popping up over and over,
but I had a feeling it was Tiny and the crew, so the calls
went unanswered. I wanted to be done with them. One
week of running around with them was enough to confirm all my thoughts about them and where they were
headed. I wasn't trying to put myself in that cell with
them, so I planned to stay as far away from them as possible. Especially after the stunt they pulled at the party.

I said my good-byes to the staff of Nya's and walked
outside to meet the driver, who was standing by the back
door of a black Lincoln Town Car.

"Madam," he said and tipped his hat to me as I stepped
into the backseat.

Barry had driven me to the salon in his Porsche convertible and I assumed he was picking me up in it, but here I was getting chauffeured around the city like a big shot. I could get used to this. I sat in the backseat and slipped my seat belt around me as the driver closed the door. The cell phone rang again and I ignored the call. I decided to check my voice mail to see if the mysterious caller had left a message.

*Trick, don't try to play Houdini on me. You done hooked up with a baller and now you wanna go and play hide-and-seek. Well, please know that I will find you. I want my cut,* Tiny's voice said. *Stevie told me you running around with a millionaire. Well, I hooked you up with that millionaire, so I'm looking for mine. You better tell Daddy Fat Pockets you need a few grand, or else.*

I couldn't hit the Delete button fast enough. Who did this chick think she was dealing with? I wanted to call her back and ask her to meet me somewhere so I could beat the brakes off of her butt. I was livid and it was evident when I looked down at my shaking hands. How dare that trick act like I owed her something when she was the one who left me somewhere, drugged up, where anything could've happened to me? Tiny had a lot of nerve. I took a couple of deep breaths when I was interrupted by the driver. "You have a call," he said.

"How do you like your hair?" Barry's voice came through the speakers.

"It's straight," I said, looking around for a speaker to talk into.

"Okay," he said with a chuckle. "Are you hungry?"

"No. I'm good. I just ate breakfast."

"That was three hours ago," he said. "Well, I'll see you shortly. The driver is taking you to my studio. I'm here, and we'll take a few shots, then get you back to the house. Okay?"

"Okay," I said, and stared back out the window.

"Also," he said, "Lola said we need to get you a tutor."

All of a sudden I became nervous and scared. What was going on? Why was this guy being so nice to me? Why was he spending all this money on me, whisking me around in Town Cars and laying out the red carpet for me? He didn't seem like he was interested in me in any kind of romantic way. As a matter of fact, he paid me very little attention. I noticed pictures around his house of a beautiful woman who appeared to be from some Spanish-speaking country. When I asked him who she was, he just said Lola. He didn't offer any more info on the mysterious Lola, and I didn't pry. The only thing he seemed interested in was taking pictures of me. The day I left his house and turned back around, he asked me a few questions about why I needed a place to stay. I gave him a quick rundown of life in the Bluff and he nodded his head and showed me to the guest room. He helped me take my bags upstairs and then went on about his business. The only time he talked to me was when he was asking if I was hungry or showing me some modeling magazine.

My cell rang again and I didn't even bother to look at the caller identification. I pushed the little green phone icon after the first ring.

"Who do you think you're threatening? I will break my foot off in your little narrow . . . what? Oh hey, Dee."

"Where are you?" my brother said.

"Riding through Buckhead in a limo. Whatcha know about that?"

"I don't know anything about that. Sophia shot her

boyfriend because she found out he was looking at you in the shower. She's locked up."

"What?" I said. "She did what?"

"She shot him," he said.

"Is he dead?"

"As far as I know," I said.

"Where is Devin?"

"He's down the street at that white lady's house."

"Mrs. Eichelberger?"

"Yeah," he said. "I'm going by there as soon as school is over."

"School? Oh, you for real, huh?"

"We need to talk. I don't know what you doing, but whatever it is, you need to stop."

"Nah," I said. "I need to keep doing what I'm doing. You have no idea how much I need to keep doing what I'm doing."

"Jasmine," he said in a frustrated tone.

Whenever he used my full name, he was pissed. It had been that way since we were little kids.

"Listen, Dee. I know what I'm doing, and even if I didn't, I'ma ride this train until it runs into a wall. I'm in no rush to get back to the Bluff."

My brother sighed and I could almost see him shaking his head.

"I'm not doing anything wrong. I'm not with Tiny and them either. I'm solo."

"Well, how in the hell are you riding around in a limo? Whatchu do, hit the lottery?"

"Something like that." I noticed that we were pulling into a parking lot. "Is this your cell phone you're calling me from?"

"Yeah," he said as if he really didn't want me to hang up.

"I'll call you tonight," I said. "I love ya, Dee. And don't worry about me. Just make sure Devin is straight."

"Yep," he said. "I hope you ain't doing nuttin' that will have you sitting in a cell beside Sophia."

"No," I said. "I'm good. I promise you that I'm not doing anything illegal."

"Well, what are you doing in a limo, Jasmine?"

"I gotta go," I said. "I'll tell you all about it tonight."

"A'ight," he said.

I hung up the phone and stepped out of the car. We were in the parking lot of what appeared to be the back of a strip mall. The driver walked with me over to a door that was painted a loud red. Before we reached the door, Barry opened it and smiled at me.

"Look at you!" he said. "You already look like a super-model. This is gonna be good. You are going to get me out of that stuffy office and I'm going to get you out of that Buff."

"Bluff," I said with a chuckle. "But it's all good."

"Come on in," he said, then turned to the driver and reached out to sign the little clipboard the man was carrying. "Thanks, bro. I'll take it from here."

I walked into the studio and was led over to an area with a single chair and a white background. There were a few umbrella-looking things covering some lights.

"Have a seat," Barry said. "I just want to get a couple of shots."

"So you are for real?" I asked, still not digesting that all of this was happening to me.

"Yes," he said, looking at me like he really didn't play games when it came to his photography. He smiled at me and gave me a little wink. He then walked over to me with this little black square thingy with a white button on it. He held the thingy up to my face and pushed a button. I heard it click, then a pop of the lights.

"What's that?"

"It's a reflector. We need to make sure the lighting is correct. This shouldn't take long. Just sit tight."

I sat down in the chair and a woman appeared. I recognized her immediately. She was the woman in the pictures at Barry's house.

"I'm Lola," she said with a pleasant smile. She walked over and extended her hand to me.

"Nice to meet you," I said, not sure what to think of the statuesque woman standing before me. She was even prettier in person.

"Let's get her in makeup," she said. "I must say, I have to agree with Barry. You have great bones."

*Great bones? What the . . . ? Did I just hook up with a bunch of cannibals?*

# 11

# DeMarco

I woke up to the sound of a fire truck wailing right out in front of my door. The truck's siren sounded just like the one they used at the detention center to alert the officials of a resident's escape. Once that horn was sounded, we were expected to sit down wherever we were and place our hands behind our heads. I rolled over off the sofa and sat on my butt with my heart racing. I didn't realize that I wasn't at the Metro until I noticed the pile of dirty clothes sitting in the chair in the corner by the front window. Once I realized I was at home, I jumped up, feeling stupid and institutionalized. A game show was on television, which meant that I was late for school. I looked at the clock on the wall and saw that it was a little past nine. School started at eight.

"Dag," I said as I rushed to the bathroom to brush my teeth and wash my face. "I guess there is no need to rush now."

After finishing up in the bathroom, I walked over to the

bag with the clothes that I had purchased at the mall and removed a pair of Levi's jeans and a red and white Hollister T-shirt. I put on my clothes, slipped my feet into my brand-new Air Max 95s, and pulled my pants down below my waist. I walked into Jasmine's room and paused. Her empty bed made me feel a sense of loss.

Where was my sister?

I sighed and closed my eyes, saying a little prayer for her to be safe wherever she was. I opened my eyes and looked in the mirror behind her bedroom door. I smiled at my own reflection. I was fresh to death, if I had to say so myself. I walked over to her dresser and used a little of her lotion on my arms and face. I used the pink brush that was sitting by the empty jewelry box to get my waves in order. I noticed a five-subject tablet and I grabbed it. I wouldn't want to show up at school after all this time without school supplies. I searched around for a pen and found one in the drawer. Once I had what I needed, I left the room. I felt weird being in the apartment alone. I don't think I could ever remember being here alone. I walked into the hallway, stepped over the blood, and entered the kitchen. The Raid must've worked because when I turned on the lights, only a few roaches were around and they were moving slow. I opened the refrigerator and pulled out the carton of orange juice. I killed the rest of it and tossed the container in the trash pile. I made a mental note to take it out to the Dumpster when I got home from school. I made my way over to my mother's room and opened the door. Her bed was still unmade, clothes were piled up in each corner, and I could still smell her scent. I wondered how she was holding up after her first night in jail. I needed to check on her once I got out of school. I closed the door and walked out the front door. I locked the door behind me and hustled down the street. I stopped at Mrs. Eichelberger's house and stuck my hand through the gate to let myself in. I went down the walk-way, up the steps to the front porch, and rang the door-bell.

Nobody answered. I pushed the button again and placed my ear to the door, listening for any sign of life in-side. Nothing. I wondered where they were at this time of morning. I was naturally paranoid anyway, and this little disappearing act didn't help ease my mind. I pulled out my cell phone and searched for the number that they gave me last night. I pushed the call icon and heard the phone ringing inside the house. Once the voice mail picked up, I hung up. I hoped these weird white folks didn't run off with my little brother. I would hate to catch a charge be-hind these hippies. I turned on my heels and hustled off the porch and back to the street.

"What's up, Dee," yelled a neighborhood guy who was standing on his porch. "You out of jail?"

"Nah," I said as I walked past him. "I'm still there."

He frowned as if my words carried more weight than his own eyes. I hated when people asked stupid ques-tions.

"Where you going? To school?" he asked.

I also hated when people asked you a question and an-swered it before you could.

"Yeah, man," I said. "I'll holla at you later."

I walked across Joseph E. Lowery Boulevard and did my speed walk until I made it to James Charles High School. I ran up the steps of the huge building and ran straight into a metal detector. I walked through it and it went off.

"Slow ya roll," said a heavyset female, whose security uniform was way too tight. "Walk back through it again and put your tablet on the table. If you got a cell phone, put that on the table too."

I did as I was told and managed to make it through without hearing the beep. I saw a group of guys from my neighborhood; they were all gang members. Normally I would go holla at them, but I was trying to stay out of trouble so I walked the other way. I went into the office and registered myself. After I got a schedule, I went to class.

James Charles was a hood school and it was off the chain. It was worse than it was when I left last year. When I walked into my class, a fight was in progress between two wild-looking girls. I turned around and walked right back out without even talking to the teacher. I had physical education on my schedule next, so I figured I would just go hang out in the gym until my class started.

"Dee," a voice called out as I made my way down the hallway.

"What's good, folk?" I said for the fifty millionth time today. It felt good to be missed, but I was tired of speaking and shaking hands. Students and teachers alike seemed to want a little bit of my time.

I stopped by the cafeteria because I saw a few familiar faces, and being that I was already skipping my first class, I figured I would go and speak. As I made my way over to a crowd of people who were oohing and aahing, I had to laugh at what I saw. In the middle of the crowd was none other than my man Jolly, spitting his whack rhymes.

"So the honey asked Jolly, can I be your mate?  .

As long as you're not straight, we can go out on a date.

I prefer my women gay; I'm freaky like dat buddy
I will relax on my back let ya rub up on my tummy."

"Man," I said, slapping him on his shoulder, "give it up."

"Deeeee," he said, turning around and hugging me as if he didn't just see me yesterday. "My man. What's good with ya? Still sleeping on the skills, huh?"

"Jolly," I said. "We're friends, right?"

"You my best friend. What's up?"

"I got some problems, bro."

"What you need?"

"My mom is in jail."

"Jail? You just got out. What she do, go in to hold your spot for ya?"

"Man," I said, "this is serious and you're over here playing."

"Okay," he said. "What is she in jail for?"

"She shot this dude she called her boyfriend."

"Wow," Jolly said. "Y'all got some violent genes in yo family."

"Forget it, man," I said, walking off.

He gave chase and pulled my shoulder to stop me.

"I'm sorry. Whatchu need a player to do?"

"I don't know, but we gotta figure out a way for this to come up as some kind of self-defense."

"Man," he said, "say no more. I'll get up on the stand and tell the judge and the jury that I saw ole boy slap the taste outta her mouth. She grabbed the gun and blasted on him."

"Jolly," I said, shaking my head, "I'm serious, dude. I don't need for you to lie. I need to borrow some of that money to get her out."

"No problem," he said, digging into the pockets of his baggy jean shorts and coming out with two big wads of cash. "Six grand right there. I need to keep a few hundred for my personal use, but that's all I have to my name."

"This is a whole lot of money for a part-time painter to have."

"You want the money or not?"

"I do," I said. "But why are you walking around with this kind of money on you?"

"Did you forget that my mother is a crackhead? You can't hide nuttin' from no crackhead, Dee. You know that. The CIA need to hire a few of them to find who killed Tupac and Biggie. A crackhead would've found that clown years ago. They would be all up in the caves with lil cigarette lighters."

"Man, you're crazy," I said as I took the money and reached out a closed fist to tap his with.

"You know I ain't lying. Crackheads are resilient, bro."

"You a fool," I said, shaking my head at my friend. "I'll get this back to you as soon as I can. When I leave here I'm going down to talk to a bail bondsman. Hopefully I can get her out of there. Moms has her problems, but she's not a criminal."

"Handle that situation, cuz. We're straight. Even though that was my studio money. But since this is a homie emergency, I can hold off on the demo for now. Family first."

I appreciated Jolly's kind gesture and I didn't expect him to do this, but I wasn't really all that surprised. Jolly was my man, and this is what the homies did for each other. I couldn't count the amount of times I'd looked after him. Back in the day, he was just a fat kid running around the Bluff and couldn't fight a lick. I stopped the bullies from making him their whipping boy and allowed him freedom to roam around the hood unmolested. I also took a charge for him once and did ninety days in the juvey for a crime he committed. This was how we got down. I looked after him and now he was coming through for me.

"Yo," he said. "Don't mean to put this on ya at a time like this, but you need to know."

"I'm listening," I said as I prepared for more bad news.

"Word is, Tiny and her crew s'posed to be pissed off at Jaz. They claim she got them for some money. They talking real reckless 'bout what they gonna do to her if she don't come through with this so-called money. Tiny is feeling herself and tryna act like she some kind of kingpin or something. She don't know I will fight a girl. I'm talking 'bout straight body slam. Bam. Right on the floor, cuzzo."

"Yeah," I said. "I wish they would lay a finger on my sister. I'll personally send them . . . anyway. I don't have time for those clowns right now. I need to take care of this business with my moms."

"I'm wit ya. I was just telling you what I was hearing. That's all," Jolly said.

"I feel ya," I said. "Thanks for the heads-up. I'll take care of them in due time."

The bell rang and Jolly and I shook hands again. He threw up two fingers and I did the same before we went our separate ways.

"Boy," Dr. Rogers, the school's principal, said as she walked her tall, slim frame over to me. "Why in the world did you put a tattoo on your handsome face?"

I smiled but didn't say anything. She licked her finger and started wiping at it as if it would go away.

"Oh, come on, Dr. Rogers," I said with a frown. "How you gonna put spit on my face?"

"Leave that alone, Doc," said a kid I didn't know as he walked by. "I'm 'bout to get me one just like it."

"No, you're not," she said. "And pull your pants up."

The kid pulled his pants up and reached out his hand to shake mine. I shook it and turned to the principal.

"How you doing, Dr. Rogers?"

"I'm fine," she said. "It's good to see you here at James Charles High."

"It's good to see you too," I said.

"I hope you're done with all that trouble?"

"Yes, ma'am," I said. "That's a thing of the past. Ready to move forward."

Dr. Rogers was always cool with me. She was fun but firm, fair but could give you a little wiggle when she saw the need. She was always dressed to the nines and carried herself with as much class as anyone I had ever met or seen on television. She wore different color framed glasses depending on what she pulled out of the closet that morning. I'm sure she could've worked anywhere, but she chose James Charles High because she said we needed each other. She always said she got more from the students than we could ever get from her, but I couldn't find where she was getting that from. Most of the students at JCH were knuckleheads from the hood and she was a polished woman who probably grew up with a silver spoon in her mouth. But then again, maybe she didn't, because I've seen her get ghetto on occasion.

"That's great to hear. Now back it up with a little action. Where is your sister? I haven't seen her in about two or three weeks."

I sighed and shook my head. "I don't know," I said.

Dr. Rogers looked at me over the top of her red frame glasses as if she were scanning my brain. She nodded her head but didn't say anything.

"I'm going to get her back up here though," I said.

"Good," she said. Dr. Rogers looked at me as if she wanted to tell me something but couldn't find the words.

"What's wrong, Dr. Rogers?"

"I want you to stay clear of trouble, DeMarco. You are a good boy with so much potential and I want you to fulfill that potential, not squander it. Do you understand?"

"Yes, ma'am," I said.

"Okay," she said. "I'm going to see what I can do, but as of right now, I'm not going to be able to let you come back to school. Your arrest happened on school premises, so you'll have to get approval from the school board before they will allow you to come back. I really hate to tell you that. I don't want to send any kid back out of my school, but my hands are tied."

"Shut the hell up, Dr. Rogers," someone said from the distance. The slight was followed by laughter from a crowd of people.

Dr. Rogers didn't even look in the perpetrator's direction. Her eyes were on me, and she looked like she was more hurt than I was.

"Okay," I said, disappointed at not being able to prove that I was ready to move beyond my past.

"If you need for me to go to the board with you, just let me know. I believe in you, DeMarco," Dr. Rogers said. She reached out and rubbed my arm. "Let me know when you are ready."

My mind was racing in ten different directions when a hand slipped by my side and looped my arm.

"Hello there, you good-looking boy," Morgan, my child-hood crush, said.

All of a sudden all my troubles seemed to float away.

"Hey," I said, looking down at the prettiest girl in the entire school. "How you doing?"

"I'm doing just fine now that I see you. I was looking for you all morning. I thought you lied to me."

"Never that. I had lots of drama at home last night and didn't go to sleep until late. I didn't wake up until after nine o'clock. So needless to say I had to hustle over here after you guys were already in class. Then I had to reregister and all that stuff. Now I hear that I can't stay. Something about my last arrest."

"What? So when can you get that cleared up?" Morgan asked, showing those perfect white teeth. "I need you to be here so you can play basketball and be with me."

"I wanna be with you too," I said, ready to go see the school board right now.

"Man," Morgan said, frowning and crossing her arms as if she were a small child throwing a tantrum.

"I'ma try to get it straight tomorrow," I said.

"Why not today?"

"I guess I can go down there today. That's if I can get my grandma to go with me."

"Okay," she said. "You need to cover up that tattoo before you go down there to that board, DeMarco. They will send your butt straight to the alternative school if they see that."

I frowned. "You don't like this, for real?"

"It's not about what I like," she said with a frown that said she hated it. "You need to get back in school, boy."

"I plan to," I said.

"Why did you put that on your face in the first place, DeMarco?"

"I made the mistake of tattooing some teardrops on my face, and we know that most people think they symbolize a body. Well, I didn't want folks who only knew what they saw on television looking at me and thinking I was a murderer, so I had to cover up the teardrops. So I did this tribal thing."

"I see," Morgan said. "Well, it is what it is. Don't know how I'ma take you home to meet my momma."

"Your momma already loves me. Thank you very much."

"Lucky you. Speaking of moms, how is Miss Sophia doing these days?"

Back to reality. My mood immediately went back to gloom and doom.

"We'll talk about that later," I said as I rolled my eyes at the task ahead of me with Sophia. "I need to get out of here and you need to get to class."

"True," Morgan said. "I like this new and improved De-Marco Winslow, so go handle your business so you can get yourself back in school, please."

She pulled me down to her face and puckered her soft lips, then allowed me to kiss her.

I was back on cloud nine.

Morgan ripped a piece of paper off the bulletin board that was behind us. She scribbled a number on it and handed it to me.

"That's my cell phone. Hit me up a little later, okay? I wanna hear what the board says."

"Will do," I said.

She gave me that lovely smile again and walked off.

I stood there in the almost empty hallway watching my sexy little tomboy-looking crush walk to her class.

She turned around, smiled, and waved at me. As much drama as I had ahead of me getting my sister and mom back home, getting the board to allow me back in school, and making sure my little brother hadn't been kidnapped, I felt good. And I had friends like Jolly and Morgan to thank for that. Life wasn't so bad after all.

# 12

## JASMINE

The photo shoot was done and I was now sitting at a table running my fingers across a crisp linen tablecloth. We were at The Palm, an upscale restaurant in the heart of Buckhead. Soft music played in the background as some of Atlanta's wealthiest people sat around their tables laughing as if they didn't have a care in the world. I recognized a few faces from television. A popular morning-show personality was sitting with his family two tables over from where we were sitting. I saw Jermaine Jackson; at least I think that was Jermaine. Maybe it was Marlon or Tito—I wasn't sure, but I knew it was one of those Jackson brothers. I picked up my menu and scanned the selection. I had no idea what these dishes were, so I figured I'd focus on the main meat ingredient. Steak, lobster, and fish—I wanted some seafood, so I decided that I would order the Shrimp Bruno. It sounded big and I was hungry. I looked at the prices that were in small print to the right of the entrées and my eyes almost popped out of my head. Were these people crazy? Seventy-five dollars for a steak? Sixty-eight dollars for a chicken-something? Yeah, they weren't wrapped too tight upstairs. No wonder some rich people ended up broke and jumping out of windows. They were crazy to begin with.

"So how did you like your first shoot?" Barry asked as he told the waiter his order.

"It was a'ight, I guess," I said. I wasn't sure how I was supposed to feel about sitting in a chair while people snapped pictures of me.

"You're a natural," he said. "Lola thinks you have what it takes to make it big. Runways as well as print. Her opinion matters to a lot of shot-callers in the business. She's really good friends with Tyra Banks. Who knows, she may be able to get you on her show."

"I don't wanna be on that show," I said.

"What? Are you serious?"

"Am I getting paid for this?" I asked after I told the waiter what I wanted.

"Excellent choice," said the young white waiter, who had too much mousse in his hair. "You are very pretty, by the way."

"Did you pay him to say that?" I asked Barry. I was from the Bluff and knew a hustle when I saw one. I've been going places since I was a little girl, and not once did I hear a waiter call me pretty.

Barry laughed.

The waiter gave me a smile before walking away.

"You're funny, you know that?" Barry said. "You are hilarious."

"And you're pouring it on a little thick. And I asked you if I was getting paid for this."

"Of course you are. I'm not that type of guy, Jasmine," he said as he stopped laughing.

He appeared to be offended, but I didn't care. All of a sudden I wasn't feeling so sure about this modeling thing. I wanted to go home. I wasn't comfortable in this setting. Everyone around me seemed stuffy and full of crap. If this was what rich people lived like, then I wasn't interested in being rich.

"I like to strike a fair deal with everybody that I work with," Barry said.

"You straight," I said, fanning him off. "I appreciate you giving me a place to stay and not trying to creep into my bed."

"You're just a baby," he said, shaking his head from side to side. "Any grown man who tries to sneak in your bed is sick and should be shot."

"My momma just shot the man who I told you about," I said nonchalantly.

Barry jerked his head back. "Did she kill him?"

I shrugged my shoulders and I really didn't care if she did or didn't. Sophia's motherly move came about five years too late.

"Is she in jail?" Barry asked.

"I guess," I said. "I don't know. I was with you."

He seemed flustered, as if he was going through some things internally. By the look on his face, you would think it was *his* mother who was the one in trouble.

"It doesn't matter," I said. "I'm done with all that crap over at that house."

"Well," Barry said and sighed while rubbing his temples, "we have two options as far as getting you out there in the business. One, you'll have to get your parents or your mom to sign a permission slip to release the photos that we have of you."

I frowned and sucked my teeth at the suggestion.

"The second option would be for you to emancipate yourself. Basically claim your own independence, and from there you can do your thing."

"I like that one a little better," I said with a smile. "But how do I emancipate myself?"

"I'm not sure, but I will have my attorney speak to you tomorrow. And we have to get you a tutor for school and some etiquette classes. If you're going to be as big as we think you are, you'll be associating with people who will expect you to carry yourself a certain way. And school. Gotta get you back in that. No need to make a million bucks and not be able to count it," Barry said.

"Why you doing all of this?"

"I told you. I believe you have the look, and I hate my job as a stockbroker. I make lots of money but I hate what I do. And a wise man once told me, in order to live your life to the fullest, you should find something that you would do for free and figure out a way to get paid for it."

"Who said I wanted to model?" I asked.

Barry sat back in his chair as if that was the last thing he expected me to say.

I stared at him, waiting on a reply. He squirmed in his chair as if he couldn't take the chance of me bailing out. As I sat there watching him, I realized that I must have something. There must be something about me that he saw in me that I didn't see in myself.

"I miss my little brother. I need to go see him," I said.

Barry nodded his head. "No problem," he said. "We can head over there after dinner."

"I'll catch MARTA," I said.

There was that frightened look again.

"Do you want to model, Jasmine?" he asked, as if the question itself was blasphemy.

"I don't mind," I said. "As long as I can take care of myself and my brothers, I'll do it. But I've heard too many crazy stories about those models getting hooked on drugs and being raped. I don't need to put on some fancy clothes and get my hair and nails done for that. I can stay in the Bluff and get hooked on drugs and raped."

"I can promise you that I won't let anything happen to you," Barry said. I believed him. He had been nothing short of a gentleman since the first time I spoke with him.

"I hear you, but . . . I don't know. I need to talk to my brother."

"Sure," he said.

Our food came and just as I was about to dig in to this too-little amount of food for the money, Lola walked in and sat down. She was wearing a pair of white-frame shades that I bet cost up in the thousands of dollars. She had on a white blouse, white tights, and a pair of silver pumps that I wanted bad. Her hair was pulled back into a ponytail, but it was still flawless.

"Great shots, girl," she said as she sat down and tossed her oversized bag in an empty chair.

"Thanks," I said as I took a bite of my shrimp. I slowed down my chewing and savored the taste. This had to be the best food I ever had in my life. Good Lord, what did they put in this stuff?

"I have a few calls in, and everyone wants to see the shots of this hot youngster. We already have *Teen 1* magazine wanting to do a cover shoot. Are you kidding me?

Girls wait for years for an opportunity like this, and you got it just like that. This is going to be great for you, girl," she said.

"I'm not sure that Jasmine's as passionate about this as we are," Barry said with that hurt puppy-dog look on his face.

Lola removed her designer shades and looked at me. "You either have it or you don't and, Jasmine, you have it, girl. So please, do yourself a favor and work it," she said, biting her bottom lip and doing some crazy dance. "I'm just saying."

I smiled. I liked Lola. I liked Barry too but he was up-tight and too much like a father. Lola acted like she had been in my shoes. We hadn't spent much time together but we seemed connected.

"She wants to catch the MARTA over to her neighborhood and check on her family," Barry said.

"Not," Lola said. "Supermodels don't ride on MARTA, unless MARTA is paying for a commercial or something of the sort."

"But I'm not a supermodel," I said.

"I wasn't talking about you," she said with a straight face, then smiled. "I was talking about me, and since I'll be going with you, I'm not getting on MARTA. Barry can drive or we'll take a car."

I laughed again and almost spit out my food.

"I'll call a car," Barry said. "I have to go and get some work done."

"What else is new," Lola said. "Girl, hurry up and eat that so we can do a little shopping and get you to your affairs with your family."

"I'll see y'all later," Barry said, standing up and leaving

most of his food on the plate. He walked around the table and kissed Lola on her forehead. He rubbed my back and walked out.

"And he left me to pick up the bill," she said. "Men. Can't live with them and you can't kill them."

"Nobody told my momma that," I said.

"Your mother killed a man? She's my shero," Lola said as she reached over and took Barry's plate and began eating his food.

I gave her a look and she gave me one back.

"I'm from the South Side of Chicago. I don't believe in wasting food."

I laughed again and knew right then and there that we were going to be okay.

# 13

## DeMarco

I walked out of the school and stood on the step of the old, antiquated building. Not too long ago I would've been sneaking out of the place to go and get into some devilment, but now I felt horrible for leaving. I was ready to get started on my new life, but the doggone school officials were still trying to punish me. I had already done the time that the judge said I had to do—now I had to jump through their red tape just to go back to school. I stood there staring out at the busy street. People were going on about their business, living their lives, and here I was on the outside looking in. I shook my head and decided I would go over to my grandmother's house. It wasn't like I had anything else to do. It was almost noon and I figured she would probably be up and sitting on the front porch. More than likely she would be in her rocking chair, waving to any- and everyone who passed by. She was getting up there in age, and I heard her health had been getting worse. I hadn't seen her in almost a year.

I left the school premises and turned to my right, headed over to Vine City. I decided to take a shortcut and walk through the parking lot of the liquor store, which was a block west of James Charles High. Just as I passed the check-cashing place, I heard something—or was it someone? I stopped walking and listened closer.

"Dee," the faint voice said.

I walked over to the sound, but couldn't find the source.

"Dee," the voice said. "Down here, man."

I looked down at the ground, in between the Check Cashing Spot and the coin laundromat. I saw a skinny figure holding his side and looking up at me with a face that was covered with blood. I did a double take when I realized that the beaten man was my friend Coo Coo. He was lying on his side, and his white T-shirt was splattered with blood and dirt. I ran over to him and tried to lift him up.

"No, no, no, nooo," he said in a pain-filled voice that stopped me from touching him. "Don't touch, Dee."

"What happened to you, man?" I said, pulling back and standing over him. "Were you shot?"

"Nah, man," he said as he rocked back and forth in pain. "Those VC fools jumped me."

He was speaking about the Vine City Hustlers, a local street gang who had been terrorizing the area for years. The only street that separated Vine City from the Bluff was Joseph E. Lowery Boulevard, and for as long as I could remember the two areas had problems with each other. The Bluff Boys was our gang, and Vine City Hustlers was theirs. I didn't care for either one of them. I was always solo, but my people were down with the Bluff Boys. Vine City Hustlers had about a hundred or so members and they made their money by intimidation and robbing people. The Bluff Boys were into drug sales and stolen goods. Vine City had a girl gang too, and they hustled men for their money. Word around town was that Tiny was the leader of the female section of the Vine City Hustlers, which was why I had to make sure my sister wasn't in with those guys.

I helped Coo Coo sit up. His face was already starting to swell.

"Why did they jump you?" I asked.

"They robbed me. I just got out today. I ain't even been home yet," Coo Coo said as he spit out a mouthful of blood. "I think my ribs broke, brah. I can barely breathe."

I pulled out my cell phone and dialed 911. I gave the operator the info she requested and hung up. My friend was in agonizing pain and I couldn't do anything to help him.

"Well, look what we have here," a guy who was about my size said as he appeared out of nowhere with two other people. All three of the boys wore blue jeans, white T-shirts, and had orange bandannas hanging out of their pockets. That was the flag of Vine City Hustlers, so I immediately knew they were trouble.

I sized up the guy who was talking. He was my height, but thin as a rail. His hair was braided back and wrapped in a white bandanna. Then there was a short one who didn't have much of a neck and was only a doughnut or two from being overweight. The third guy had a pale complexion and seemed to have a few muscles. I didn't know him, but I recognized Mr. Muscles from one of my stays at Metro. I figured they were carrying weapons, so a fair fight was out of the question.

"I'm just trying to get my man home," I said.

"Nobody asked you nuttin'," Short-and-Fat said.

I stared at the little guy and could see the word *coward* written all over his face. His confidence came from his two comrades, but without them I could tell he wouldn't bust a grape with Welch's permission.

"Whatcha got on ya, boy?" the one with the braids said as he eyed my pockets.

"Flat broke," I said and slapped the front of my pants for effect. "I just came home."

"You looking pretty fresh for somebody who just came home," Short-and-Fat said.

I hunched my shoulders but didn't say anything.

"Empty your pockets, boy," Braids said. "You know what time it is. VC boys on the scene. Give it up."

I wasn't about to give these clowns the six thousand dollars that Jolly loaned me. They would have to kill me before I let that happen.

"I don't have nuttin' to give ya, homie," I said.

"I ain't ya homie. Bluff Boys ain't built real enough to be my homeboy, ya dig?" Short-and-Fat snapped.

Braids walked over to me and reached down to touch my pocket. The fact that there were three of them and just one of me made me a little uncomfortable. As soon as Braids's hand brushed up against my jeans, I hit him with a right cross to his jaw. It was a solid punch and his knees buckled; then I followed with a left cross to his temple.

*Bam.*

That punch did the trick and he was pretty much out on his feet. I reached out and grabbed him before he could fall to the ground. I had a feeling that Short-and-Fat and Mr. Muscles would pull out their guns, which they did. But they were too late and weren't that bright. I flipped Braids around so that his back was on my chest and wrapped my arm around his neck. I tightened my grip as if I was trying to pop his eyes out of his head. If his friends were going to shoot me, then they would more than likely hit him. I had a feeling they didn't spend much time at the shooting range. I used my free hand to feel around his waist to see if he was packing a pistol. He wasn't.

"Let him go," Short-and-Fat said with his voice cracking like a girl, holding his gun sideways with an unsteady hand. He was afraid, but he still had his gun and that concerned me. A scared man was very dangerous. I remained cool.

"Let my people go before I bust a cap in your head, boy," Short-and-Fat yelled, loud enough for anyone to hear.

"Let me see how good you can shoot," I said calmly. I tightened my grip on Braids because he was the only thing between me and a few bullets. My victim's body was going limp under my choke hold.

"Boy, you crazy?" Mr. Muscles said and smiled at me. Then as if he had a great idea, he pointed his little pistol at Coo Coo. "If you don't let him go, I'ma kill your home-boy."

"And I will kill yours," I said, tightening my grip around Braid's neck. "The choice is yours."

I didn't mean to throw Coo Coo under the bus or play games with his life, but this was kill or be killed and I wasn't dying.

"Y'all better put those guns down or I will snap his neck." I whispered into Braid's ear, "You need to talk to your boys."

I released my grip enough for my victim to speak.

"P-P-P-Puuuuuuutt'em down. Go ahead," Braids said through his quickly closing windpipe. "He gonna kill me, y'all."

They did as they were told.

"Kick 'em over by that trash can," I said, not releasing my grip one inch.

The ambulance that I had called a few minutes ago showed up. A few seconds later a police car pulled in behind them. Short-and-Fat and Mr. Muscles took off running.

I continued to choke my prey. He was losing his fight for life and I wasn't in any rush to give him a reprieve, but the ambulance had parked, so I relaxed my grip. I wasn't trying to catch a murder case behind this fool. The two paramedics were out of their vehicle and headed our way. I turned Braids around to face me. He tried to bend over to catch his breath, but I wouldn't let him.

"I know this isn't over, but it better be," I said. "My name is DeMarco. They call me Dee. I want you to know the name of the man who let you live. You got that? I let you live," I said.

Braids nodded his head while holding his neck. The police and the paramedics were getting closer. I patted him on his back and motioned with my head for him to follow his friends. He coughed a few times to catch his breath, then stumbled off down the alley. I watched him as he ran and held his neck. He never looked back, but I knew I would see him again.

"Is he okay?" one of the emergency-tech guys said, pointing at the gang member who was slowly picking up speed.

"Oh yeah. He's fine," I said and turned to my friend Coo Coo. "He's the one who needs help."

"Where is he running off to?" an old black police officer said as he walked up. He looked like he should be retired instead of responding to petty crimes.

"He gotta get back to school," I said. "I guess the late bell is about to ring."

"Looks like you guys were fighting," the police officer said and gave me a funny look.

"Fighting?" I said with a frown as if he had misread the situation. "Nah. That's my homeboy. We were just messing around."

"Yeah, okay," he said. I could tell he didn't believe me, but I didn't care. "What happened to him?" the officer asked, motioning toward Coo Coo.

"Somebody jumped him," I said.

The officer shook his head, huffed as if he was so tired of my kind, and walked back to his car. I thought he was going to sit down and fill out a report or something, but he started his car and pulled off.

I stood still and watched the paramedics place Coo Coo on the stretcher and wheel him to the ambulance. Once my friend was taken care of, I retrieved the Vine City boys' weapons. I placed them in the waistband of my jeans and covered them with my shirt. I hated the fact that I was going to have to deal with those clowns, but oh well. I didn't do anything but defend myself, so whatever happened was going to happen. Either way, I wasn't sweating it.

I continued on my way to my grandmother's house, which was back across Joseph E. Lowery Boulevard. I had to pass my street, so I decided to try Mrs. Eichelberger's house again. I let myself in the gate and knocked on the door again. Nothing.

Maybe they took Devin to the zoo or something. I was sure they didn't leave this nice house to kidnap a little boy from the hood. If that's what they were after, they could've knocked on about fifty doors and just asked for one.

I left the yard and walked past my apartment. I shot a look over there and couldn't help but wonder how my mother was doing and where my sister was.

As I came to the end of my street, I passed the corner store and saw Kenny, a neighborhood guy, on the corner talking to an old bum. Kenny used to be a high school football stud who was highly recruited by most of the major colleges throughout the country, but he was dumb as a brick and couldn't pass the SAT or ACT. He was now a member of the Bluff Boys and spent his days selling drugs on the corner.

"Kenny," I said, walking over to him.

"What's up, folk," he said, reaching out and slapping my hand. "Whatcha know good?"

"I got something for ya," I said as I motioned for him to follow me to the side of the building. I removed the guns and handed them to him. "Merry Christmas and happy birthday. Don't say I never gave you nuttin'."

"Cool," he said, smiling from ear to ear. " 'Preciate it, folk. What I owe you?"

"You straight," I said. "I got 'em from some Vine City clowns who tried to rob Coo Coo."

"Coo Coo?" he said. "I thought he was locked up. I thought you was locked up too."

"Obviously we're out, Kenny," I said.

"Yeah, I guess so. How you get these boys' pieces?"

"I had to choke one of 'em out, and the other two ran like punks. But I made them give me those guns before they bailed."

"They so weak over there," Kenny said, shaking his head. "You know you always been Bluff family, but we can make it official whenever you want." Kenny held both his hands wide as if welcoming me to join the Bluff Boys gang.

"And you know I don't get down like that. I run solo," I said. "I need to get out of here, bro. You take care of yourself and try not to hurt yourself with those things."

"I'ma come holla at cha this week. I need a new tat," he said.

"Anytime," I said.

"I'ma tell the boys to look out for ya. You know they gonna be looking for ya, so stay away from over on their side for a little while. They know better than to come round here," he said, then looked at his newly acquired and ill-gotten gains.

"A'ight," I said and made my way toward my grandma's house.

Just as I predicted, my grandmother, Harriet Winslow, was on the front porch waving in her rocking chair. My uncle Moochie was standing in the front yard and looking the hot mess that he was. The man had to be at least forty-five years old and, with the exception of an occasional trip to prison for his various crimes, he had never lived anywhere except with his mother. He was also delusional. It had to be a hundred degrees outside, but he had on a red, old-school Adidas warm-up suit with white stripes down the arms and legs of the jacket and pants. He wore a pair of matching red shell-toe Adidas shoes with the same white stripes. And to top off his ensemble, he wore a red terry cloth Kangol hat with a white kangaroo on the front. This fool was truly stuck in the eighties. The sad part about Uncle Moochie was he was really a nice guy. And I had never heard that he had anything wrong with his head, but the older I got the more I realized that something had to be wrong with the man.

"What's good with ya, Unk?" I said, reaching out to shake his hand.

"What's the haps, youngsta," he said and rubbed the gray patches of hair growing from his chin. "I'm just out here getting ready for this show I got to do tomorrow night," he said, staring down at a notepad.

For as long as I could remember, Uncle Moochie was headed to a show. No one had ever seen him perform, but he always claimed to be getting ready for some sort of big extravaganza.

"Oh yeah," I said. "I know you gonna kill it. Just don't dive in the crowd."

He chuckled, then looked back down at his pad as if he was really studying his rhymes. If having gray hair wasn't a sign that it was time to leave hip-hop alone, I didn't know what was.

"Hi, Grandma," I said as I walked up the steps to the old raggedy house that was in dire need of a total makeover. I opened the screen door and walked onto the porch. "How you doing, pretty lady?"

"Oh my gawd," she said, and tried to lift her heavy body up, but it was a losing battle. She gave up and held out her hands for me to come and give her a hug. "When you get home?"

"Yesterday," I said as I wrapped my arms around her neck.

"You too good of a boy to be getting in so much trouble all the time. You oughta be ashamed of yoself," she said, holding me tight.

She chastised me with the same words every time I came home from a trip to the juvey.

"I'm done with that."

"That's what you always say," she said.

"I'm for real this time," I said.

"Yeah, right," Uncle Moochie said from the yard. "I'll believe that when I see it."

"You hush your mouth, Moochie," Grandma said. "You need to worry about staying out of yo own trouble. You cast your stone when you stop yo own sinning."

"I was talking to Dee, Ma," Uncle Moochie said with a frown.

"And I was talking to you. Now hush yo mouth," she said.

"How have you being doing, Grandma?" I said after taking a seat in the rocking chair beside her.

"I'm just hanging in there. Gawd willing I'll be here tomorrow."

"Oh, come on now. You know you'll live forever."

"I don't know if I wanna live forever," she said with a chuckle. "That thing right there tryna drive me crazy with all that racket round here all the time."

"It ain't racket," Moochie said.

"It sure ain't no music, I'll tell you that much," Grandma said.

"It is music, Ma. See, that's the problem—y'all don't

support me," Uncle Moochie said with the frown of a spoiled child.

I looked at my uncle, who was nothing more than a big kid. Never mind being a nice guy, I was beginning to wonder if the man was mildly retarded. I mean, what forty-five-year-old man still lived with his mother, wrote raps on a tablet, and pranced around the front yard all day rehearsing for a show that was never going to happen?

"Well, I don't know where else you can live for free, eat for free, sleep for free. You don't even pay for the paper you wipe your lil narrow butt with, so hush," Grandma snapped at Uncle Moochie. She turned to me and shook her head.

"Oh, you gonna bring that up," Uncle Moochie said. "Okay. I'll move. I'ma get my own place."

"Yo momma called me. You know she in jail. They say she shot somebody," Grandma said to me as she rolled her eyes at Moochie.

"Yeah," I said. "So I've heard. I was there last night when they took her."

"He ain't die though. I suppose that's a good thing," she said. "I suppose."

"That's good. At least she doesn't have a murder charge," I said. "I was gonna go and see if I can get her out."

"You got money?"

"Yes, ma'am," I said. "I can take care of that part."

"How much you got?" Moochie asked from the yard. "You wanna invest in some studio time for me? Be like my executive producer or something?"

"Nah. I'm straight," I said.

"See, that's the problem," he spat. "Nobody wanna sup-

ON THE COME UP

port my dreams. When I make it big y'all gonna be the main ones all up in my face. You would rather spend some money to get my drunk sister out—"

"Shut ya mouth, Moochie," my grandmother yelled at her son. "One more word and I'ma get out this chair and slap that dumb-looking hat off your head. Don't nobody owe you nuttin'. Now shut up."

I turned to Grandma, whom I had never even heard raise her voice, never mind threaten bodily harm.

"You sure got the right nickname, 'cause you ain't nuttin' but a doggone moocher," she said.

Uncle Moochie stood there staring at his mother as if she had lost her mind. It looked like he wanted to cry. I had to stifle a laugh.

"Grandma," I said, "I need two favors."

"I only need one, but you go first," she said.

"I'm going to go in the house and make a few phone calls, and if my mom has a bail, I'ma need for you to go with me to the bail bondsman."

"We need to leave her in there for a few weeks. Let her dry out. Jail is just as good as rehab. Especially since she won't ever check herself into one. Leave her in jail for a little while," she said.

"That's not a bad idea," I said. "The second favor is to go with me to the school board. I got kicked out because I had a knife on school grounds the last time I got arrested. Now in order for me to get back in, I have to have a hearing."

"You wanna go to school? That's good, DeMarco. I'm proud of you, but I'ma have to send Moochie up there with you. I can't get round like I used to," she said.

"Okay," I said and turned to look at my uncle. He was

walking back and forth as if he was performing on a stage in a packed coliseum. I shook my head. I guess I needed to start looking into getting a GED.

"What kind of favor do you need from me, Grandma?"

"I need for you to change my Pampers for me," she said, and reached out a hand for me. "Now help me up."

# 14

## JASMINE

"Stop," I said to the driver of the black Town Car.
"Stop right here."

I noticed my little brother playing in the front yard of
the Eichelberger's house. I was so excited to see him that
I almost jumped out of the vehicle before the driver had
come to a complete stop.

"Hey, buddy," I said as I ran around the back of the car
and up to the gate.

Mrs. Eichelberger was sitting on the front porch dipping a little plastic stem into a purple bottle. She pulled
the stem out and blew some bubbles. Devin chased them
and popped them. When he saw me he turned and ran to
the gate. Mrs. Eichelberger stood and walked over to open
the gate.

"Wow," she said, looking at me like I was a foreigner.
"You look totally different, Jasmine. I didn't even know
who you were."

"How you doing, Mrs. Eichelberger?"

"I'm great. A little tired. This little guy had me running around the entire city today."

"Oh yeah," I said, and leaned down to give my little brother a hug. It felt like ages since I had seen him. "What are you doing, buddy?"

"Catching bubbles," he said with a smile. "You look funny."

"I look funny? You look funny," I said and tickled his stomach. I walked over and sat on the front steps.

"Oh no," Mrs. Eichelberger said. "You'll mess up your pants. Let me get you a chair."

"I'm good," I said, fanning her off as Devin came and stood between my legs. He was smiling at me and I was smiling right back.

"I was about to go inside and get dinner started. You wanna join us?"

"Nah," I said. "I just wanted to come over here and see Devin. Have you seen DeMarco?"

"Not since last night when he dropped Devin off. I saw on the caller ID where he called, but he didn't leave a message."

"I'll find him," I said. "I need to go by my house and get my things."

"So what are you doing with yourself these days? You look like a million bucks."

"I'm doing a little modeling," I said, and the words felt like a lie leaving my mouth. And by the look on Mrs. Eichelberger's face, she didn't believe me.

"I see," she said. "Well, I was going to get Devin started at this school tomorrow."

I looked at my little brother, who smiled when he heard

the word *school*. I wanted to take him with me, but I knew
I couldn't. I hated my mom for putting him in this position. We looked like trifling people for pawning our little
brother off on these white people.

"I'm not sure how long he'll be over here, but that's
cool. He needs to be in school. I'm working on some
things and I may be able to come get him out of your hair
in the next week or so."

"It's truly no rush. We are really enjoying his company,"
she said.

"Yeah, but he's my brother and we don't freeload off of
people," I said.

"Oh, we look at this as nothing of the sort. We're
friends, and that's what friends do."

"Yeah, and I appreciate that, Mrs. E, but that's how I
feel. I like paying my own way."

"I understand," Mrs. Eichelberger said, dropping her
head and wringing her hands. She looked sad.

"I'm going with you, Jaz?" Devin asked.

"Not today, but soon," I said. "Okay?"

"Okay," he said and walked away to play with his car.

"How much money do we owe you, Mrs. E?" I asked.
"This little guy will eat you out of house and home."

"You don't owe me anything," she said. "We have more
than enough."

I stood up and then leaned down and gave my little
brother a big hug. "I missed you, man."

"I missed you too." Devin smiled, showing off his
cavity-filled smile.

"You need to go to the dentist, boy," I said, then turned
to Mrs. E. "No candy for him, okay?"

"Okay." She turned to Devin. "You heard that, Devin.

No more candy for you, buddy. I can take him to the dentist if you like."

"That's fine, but we will pay for whatever it costs," I said. "I need to run. Give me another hug, buddy."

Devin and I hugged and said our good-byes. I walked over and hugged Mrs. Eichelberger too. She was a nice lady and I wanted her to know that I appreciated her.

I walked out the gate and over to the Town Car. The driver jumped up and grabbed my door for me. I sat inside and was glad that Lola had decided not to come. My eyes were filled with tears. Something didn't seem right about leaving my little brother with a stranger. I felt like I was leaving him at foster care or someplace.

The driver drove the fifty or so yards down to our apartment and stopped. I jumped out without waiting on him to get the door. I used my key to open the front door and was stopped dead in my tracks by the stench of the place.

"Good Lord," I said, covering my nose. "What in the heck died in here?"

Our apartment has always been a mess, but I saw that the sofa was flipped over, and the television was on the floor, broken into a bunch of pieces. Sophia and her sorry man must've had a heck of a fight.

I walked into the apartment but didn't close the door behind me. The place had a putrid odor as if some rodent had found a corner and died. I stepped over the debris and noticed a spattering of blood on the floor and wall. I stared at the damage my mother had done to that sorry man and was happy for it. I walked to my bedroom and opened the door. I stopped and sighed. My room was tossed about as well. The bed was turned over and the mattress and box spring were up against the wall. My dresser was pushed onto its side and the mirror was broken. I looked down and tried not to step on any glass as I wondered what had happened in this house. All of my clothes were piled on the floor inside of the bed frame and they were soaking wet. I could feel myself losing control of my emotions and I wanted to scream.

"Welcome home, trick," a voice said from behind me.

I turned and stared into the face of Tiny. Standing behind the short girl was Shemika.

"Don't you look nice? You didn't look like that before you jumped your lil tail in my truck. Now did you?"

I stood there staring at the girl. Here I was, standing in the middle of everything I had that was now ruined, and she was talking crazy.

"You know what you look like, Jasmine? You look like you've been running around with a rich man. A rich man I hooked you up with. So now I have a question. Where's my money?" Tiny said.

All of a sudden things started clicking in my head.

"Did you do this?" I said, motioning to the mess in my room.

"Aww yeah," she said with a smile. "I tried to help decorate the place a little bit. It was such a mess."

I reached back and punched her in her eye so hard I thought that my hand was broken. Tiny yelled and fell back into the wall.

"Get her," Tiny said, holding her eye. "Oh my God, get that trick."

Shemika did as she was told and rushed me. I swung at her and hit her in the side of the head, but as I backed up to get a little space I tripped over the bed rail and my four-inch heels wouldn't allow me to catch my balance. I fell back into the pile of wet clothes. The big girl landed on top of me with a thud. She was fat and I wasn't moving under her weight, but I swung my arms to try to get some punches into her face. We were twisting and turning with both of us trying to get some leverage on each other, but I was losing this battle. I dug my nails into her neck, but she didn't move. The big girl pushed her chin down into my chest, and that hurt. I punched some more, but she seemed to be trying to open up a hole in my chest with her chin. She was strong and I wasn't doing much to get her fat butt off of me. She pulled off of the chin attack long enough to place her fat hands around my neck. She applied pressure. I reached up and scratched at her neck, but she had all the leverage. I stopped trying to choke her and started swinging at her neck and face. I was trying to make contact with anything that would force her to release my neck, but nothing was working.

I reached down and took off my shoe and hit her in the side of her head with the heel and she made a moaning sound. I noticed that her grip had loosened up. Since that seemed to work, I hit her again and this time she fell over. I pushed the big girl off me and rolled over onto her. I straddled her and had a punching fest on her face. I grabbed her neck, lifted her head, and slammed it down as hard as I could onto the hard tile floor. Just as I lifted her head for another pounding, I felt something sharp hit my side. I immediately grabbed my side and felt the blood rushing down my hand. I turned around and noticed that Tiny had a bloody knife in her hand. I felt myself getting weaker, but I stood and went after the girl. She backed away into the hallway. I reached out to grab her, but I lost my ability to walk, stumbled, and fell face-first onto the bloody floor. I rolled over onto my back and stared into the ugly face of Tiny.

"That was for messing with my money," she said as she stood over me with a sinister-looking smile on her face. "And make sure you tell your brother that he has the same thing coming. And I still want my money."

I was gasping for air and holding my side, which felt like it was on fire. I felt myself getting dizzy. The blood was oozing through my fingers and mixing with the blood that was already on the floor. The next thing I knew I was blacking out. I felt something hit my face, but it didn't really hurt. I closed my eyes and everything went blank.

# 15

## DeMarco

There was a black car parked out in front of our apartment and I noticed a white man leaning on the trunk smoking a cigarette. I walked up to him and smiled.

"You waiting on somebody, my man?" I asked the man, who was wearing a black suit, white shirt, and black tie.

The white man dropped the cigarette and stepped on it. He looked at me and nodded his head. I could tell he wasn't afraid of being in the hood because he didn't seem nervous at all.

"Yeah," he said, then pointed to my front door. "A young lady who lives there. She been inside for about twenty or thirty minutes and we need to go. Do you know her?"

"If she lives there, it's my sister," I said. "Where do you call yourself taking her?"

He threw up his hands. "I was hired to bring her here and then take her to another location."

I nodded my head at him and started walking toward

the apartment. I gave the car a once-over and couldn't help but wonder what Jaz was doing riding around in a Lincoln.

I walked into the apartment and my eyes went straight to my sister, lying on the hallway floor. I ran over to her, but her eyes were closed and she wasn't moving. I reached out and shook her shoulders.

"Jaz," I said, still shaking her. "Jaz, wake up, girl. Who did this to you? Come on, Jaz, talk to me."

Nothing.

I looked down and saw all this blood on the floor. It was all over her clothes and the knees of my jeans. I slapped at my sister's face, but she didn't move.

"Daaaamn," I yelled and jumped up. I ran to the front door and yelled at the white guy in the black suit. "Call 911. I think somebody shot my sister."

The white guy's eyes bulged and he whipped his cell phone from his pocket. He punched the numbers into his phone and started talking. I turned around and ran back inside of the apartment. I decided that we were going to take her to the hospital. I wasn't about to let my sister die while I waited on an ambulance to show up. They were notoriously slow when they got calls from the Bluff. I leaned down and picked my sister up. Blood was every-where and I was praying that I didn't lose her as I rushed from our place.

"Open the door," I yelled at the driver. "We gonna take her to the hospital. Come on—move!"

The driver hustled to the back door and opened it. He helped me get Jaz situated across the backseat.

"Come on, Jaz," I said as I closed my eyes and asked God to spare her life. "Hang in there, girl."

My prayers were instantly answered as I heard her moan. I jumped in the front seat of the car and turned around, sitting on my knees to look at my sister. Her face was folding into a painful frown. She opened her eyes, then closed them.

"Come on, man." I turned to the white guy and was almost forced into the backseat as he sped off.

I held on to the seat as the white guy drove like he was on the run from the police. He drove like a madman toward Grady Memorial and I appreciated every stop sign and light that he ran. I also appreciated the fact that he got on the phone and alerted the emergency room that we were coming.

We arrived at the emergency room of the hospital and slammed on the brakes. Two emergency-room technicians ran out of the sliding doors with a gurney. I jumped out and opened the back door, then moved out of their way.

They got Jasmine out of the car and onto the gurney and wheeled her inside of the building. I wanted to go inside with her, but I knew they weren't going to do anything but tell me to wait outside or in the waiting room. I had come to the emergency room with more than my share of friends. I took a deep breath and tried to gather myself. I placed both my hands behind my head and interlocked my fingers and tried to breathe. I walked a few paces, then turned around and walked back. The driver of the Lincoln came over and nodded at me.

"Are you okay, my friend?" he asked while looking into my eyes.

"Yeah," I said with a deep sigh.

"This place has the best emergency room in the country. She's in good hands. I can assure you of that," he said.

"I guess when it rains it pours. First my mother shoots somebody and gets locked up. Now I come home to find my sister lying on the floor bleeding to death. What's next?"

"Hang in there, man," he said and placed his hand on my shoulder. "Everything will work out."

"Hey," I said, realizing that I hadn't asked him any questions. "Did you see who went into my house with my sister?"

"Two girls went in after her," he said. "I just figured they were her friends. They weren't inside but five, maybe ten minutes."

"And you didn't hear the gunshot?"

"There was no gunshot," he said. "Unless they used a silencer. Was she shot?"

"I thought so—maybe she was stabbed," I said. "What did these girls look like?"

"One of them was short and the other was pretty big. The big one had on a pair of jean shorts and a tank top. I thought she was a guy, but when she came back out of the apartment I got a good glimpse of her face."

"And the short one?" I asked. "Did you get a good look at her?"

"Not really, but I heard the big one call her Tiny or Teeny," he said.

"Tiny," I said. "And the big butch-looking fool was Shemika."

My heart threatened to beat its way out of my chest. How dare these lowlifes do this to my sister? They were going to pay and they were going to pay dearly for ever crossing me. I knew that minute that I was going back to jail, and this time I wasn't getting out because those girls were going to stop breathing.

"Thanks for the info, man," I said. I reached into my pockets and pulled out two twenties and handed them to him. "I promise you that I will deal with those clowns."

"Nah," he said, holding up his hands to refuse the money. "You don't owe me anything, man. I'm glad I could help."

"At least get your car cleaned," I said, still trying to give him the money.

"That's not my car, man," he said. "I just work for them. I gotta write a report anyway. Client got sick and I had to bring her to the hospital. Save your money, dude. You're fine. But can I give you some advice?"

"Go ahead," I said.

"Call the police. I know there is this 'no snitching' or 'stop snitching' thing, but forget that, man. You know who did this, so call the police and tell them."

"Nah," I said. "I'll handle it."

He frowned and hunched his shoulders as if he was expecting that response. "Well, I'll do it. You just told me that their names were Tiny and Shemika. So I'll call. I'm not bound by some dumb street code."

"Yeah, I hear ya," I said, and reached out to shake his hand.

I walked through the sliding doors of the emergency room and saw people everywhere. Grady's emergency room had to be the busiest place in Georgia. I looked around and saw a Hispanic-looking woman sitting at a desk. She was the only one who seemed to have a minute to talk.

"They just brought my sister in here," I said. "Where is she?"

"Who just brought her in?" she asked, and I noticed that her name tag said L. Gomez.

"We just pulled up and two guys came out and wheeled her in here. Her name is Jasmine and she had on all-white but was covered in blood," I said.

"Oh," she said, nodding her head. She handed me a clipboard with a stack of forms on it. "You'll have to wait out here because she's in being worked on. And being that you are related to her, you can start filling out this paperwork. Do you know if she has insurance?"

I shook my head and grabbed the clipboard.

"You can find a seat over there while you work on that. Bring it back to me once you're done," she said.

"When can I see my sister?"

"When they call for the relative of . . . what is her name?"

"Jasmine Winslow," I said.

"Thank you for that information," she said. "Fill that out as best you can. And I'll run in the back to check on her for you, okay?"

"Thanks," I said.

I stood and walked over to an empty chair and sat down. The only lines I could fill out for Jasmine were her name, address, and date of birth. I didn't know her height, weight, social security number, or what if anything that she was allergic to. I had no idea if Sophia covered us with her Medicare or Medicaid. I placed the clipboard on my lap and just sat there.

I waited and waited and waited some more.

As I sat there looking around at all the faces that were

waiting on their loved ones, I felt alone and I couldn't remember if I'd ever remembered feeling this way. I had
been placed in solitary confinement while wearing nothing but my identification bracelet, and yet I didn't remember feeling this lonely.

I closed my eyes and started talking to God.

*If you let my sister live, I promise you I will walk the
straight and narrow. I will do what I have to do to get
back in school and I'll keep my grades up. She doesn't de-
serve to die, God. Please let her live. I know I haven't
been the best person, but I'm a good person and all I'm
asking you is to let her live.*

I had been sitting in the same spot for over an hour and
I was beginning to get a little restless. I pulled out my cell
phone and dialed Morgan's number. Her voice mail
picked up so I tried Jolly and got his voice mail as well.

I stood and walked over to the Gomez lady and handed
her the clipboard. "I couldn't fill out much, but I did what
I could. Did you check on my sister?"

She took the clipboard and placed it on her desk.

"Yes," she said. "She's in critical condition right now, so
it's touch-and-go. She lost a lot of blood. All we can do
now is sit tight and wait."

My heart hit the floor. I couldn't believe what she had
just said to me.

*Jasmine was in critical condition?*

I walked outside of the emergency room to get some
fresh air and to try to digest what Mrs. Gomez had just
told me. Maybe she had the wrong person. As I was standing there pacing back and forth on the sidewalk, I saw a
white Range Rover pull up and park. I kept my eyes on the
truck and thought about Mr. P. I opened my phone and re-

alized that I hadn't put his number in my address book. I dialed 411 for information and got the number for Metro.

Officer Whiting answered the phone.

"Officer Whiting," I said, "this is DeMarco. I'm tryna get in touch with Mr. P."

"Well, hello to you too, DeMarco. You can't speak? You just call here acting like I'm your secretary or something," she snapped.

"I'm sorry. I'm in the emergency room. My sister got stabbed and I need to talk to Mr. P," I said.

"Oh. I'm sorry. Hold on a second. I just saw him walk by." Officer Whiting put the phone down and I heard her yell for Mr. P.

"Hello," Mr. P said. "What's going on, Dee?"

"I don't know, man," I said. "Some girls stabbed my sister and I feel like I'ma do something to them. I'm trying to stay out of trouble, but I feel myself losing it, man."

"Where are you?"

"I'm standing outside the emergency room at Grady," I said.

"I'm on my way. Stay there until I get there, DeMarco. Don't leave," he said, and I could hear the sense of urgency flowing from his mouth.

The phone went dead in my ear. I took a few deep breaths and felt myself calming down a little.

The cell phone rang and I looked at the screen.

"Hey," I said into the mouthpiece.

"This is Morgan," the voice said. "What's up? You talk to the people about getting back in school?"

"Nah," I said. "I didn't get a chance to. I'm at the emergency room at Grady. Some girls stabbed Jaz."

"Oh no," Morgan said. "Is she gonna be okay?"

"I don't know. The people say it's touch-and-go. I hope so. Right now she's in critical condition."

"Do you want me to come up there with you?"

"Nah," I said, "I'm straight. I just wanted to hear your voice."

"That's good because I've been thinking about you all day," she said. "DeMarco?"

"Yeah," I said.

"Please promise me that you won't do anything stupid."

"I'm not going to do anything stupid."

"Let me rephrase that, because I'm sure you don't think killing whoever did this to your sister is stupid. Don't do anything that will take you away from me again."

Her words had an effect on me. I knew Morgan liked me and I always liked her. We used to spend hours on the phone with each other, but before we could make anything official, I would always do something stupid.

"I promise," I said.

"My mom is pulling up to pick me up, so I need to go, but I will call you tonight, okay?"

"Okay," I said.

"I miss you, man," Morgan said.

"I miss you too. Hey," I said before she could hang up, "have you seen Jolly around there?"

"He's out on the courts playing ball. You want me to tell him to call you?"

"Yeah," I said. "Thanks, and make sure you call me later."

"Okay," she said. "I'll keep Jaz in my prayers and I'm sorry that this happened."

I walked over to the side of the building and took a seat

on the bench. I watched a few of the hospital employees who were outside gathered around smoking and talking.

My cell phone rang again and it was Jolly.

"What's up," I said. "Get somewhere where you can talk."

"I'm good. I'm out here by myself."

"Tiny and Shemika stabbed Jaz," I said. "I'm trying my best to stay out of trouble, but I can't let this ride, man."

"Let it ride, man," he said.

I was surprised to hear Jolly speaking like this. He was always ready to get into some foolishness.

"What happened with you and the Vine City Hustlers?" he asked.

News sure did travel fast in the hood.

"Nuttin'," I said. "I took their guns because they robbed Coo Coo and tried to rob me. I wasn't letting it go down like that."

Jolly laughed. "Okay. They were up to the school talking crazy. One of them had a black eye and he was walking around showing off. I guess he thinks it made him look tough."

"Anyway," I said, "I gotta figure a few things out, man. As long as my sister lives, I'll let it ride. If she doesn't, I'ma bring down so much pain they will wish they were never born. I can promise you that."

"God ain't gonna let Jaz die. He knows we gonna get married and have lots of little Jollys and one little Jaz."

"Whatever, man," I said, not in the mood for Jolly and his jokes today. "I'll hit you up later."

I hung up with Jolly and sat on the bench for a few more minutes. I saw a black Ranger Rover pull up and I stood. Mr. P got out of the truck and did a speed-walk up to the front entrance. He was sharp as usual. He had on a pair of gray linen pants, a black collared shirt and a pair of black sandal-looking shoes.

"Mr. P," I called out.

He stopped walking and turned to me. He changed his course and came toward me.

"Are you okay?" he asked.

"Yeah," I said. "Thanks for coming."

"Thanks for calling. That was a real smart thing to do. I'm proud of you for that, DeMarco. You're starting to think before you react."

"I don't know, Mr. P," I said as I felt myself tearing up. "I'm not feeling very smart. I know who stabbed my sister and I want revenge."

"That's only natural, DeMarco, but you have to maintain your composure, son," he said. "Let's go inside and check on your sister."

We walked inside and Mr. P went over to the same lady I spoke with, and all of a sudden she was very chatty. She was smiling from ear to ear. Then she said we could follow her. Mr. P gave me a wink and we walked through a set of double doors. Mrs. Gomez led us to this curtained off area. Mr. P stopped and motioned for me to go on behind the curtain.

I walked into the area and saw my beautiful sister lying on a bed. She had a tube running down her throat and a few other wires were connected to her. She looked so pretty lying there like Sleeping Beauty. I looked at the machine that was connected to her and it had a steady beep. I wasn't a doctor, nor had I ever stepped foot in a medical school, but I knew that the beeping was her heartbeat. I looked up to the ceiling and closed my eyes.

*Thank you, God.*

The beeping was music to my ears. I walked over and touched Jaz's arm. She was warm, and I also knew that was a good thing. Especially after having lost so much blood. I leaned down and kissed her hand and told her that I was gonna be there for her. I don't know if she could hear me or not, but I had to let her know.

# 16

## DeMarco

I sat at the table between Mr. P and his son, Blake. I found out that Blake wasn't his biological son, but Mr. P had married his mom when Blake was like five or six years old. I had to admit I was envious. I wished somebody like Mr. P had married my mom, but then again, I wouldn't wish Sophia on my worst enemy.

We were at Benihana's and I was staring mesmerized at the skills of the chef.

"Dad," Blake said, "DeMarco said he can do tattoos. Can I get one?"

"Sure," Mr. P said. "As soon as you turn thirty. When you turn thirty, Blake, you can get whatever you want."

I laughed and Blake did too.

"Thanks for checking those people out for me, Mr. P," I said, referring to a man and woman who came up to Grady to check on Jasmine. They seemed nice enough, but I didn't trust anybody.

It was two days ago when Jasmine was stabbed, and she

ON THE COME UP 157

was out of intensive care and in a regular room. The man named Barry and the woman named Lola insisted that she be moved out of Grady and into Northside. They said Grady was the best at burns and emergency situations, but they sucked once you were out of the woods. And since they agreed to pay for everything, I didn't fight with them.

"They seem like very nice people, but I understand your concern. Looks like Jaz will make a full recovery," he said.

"Thank God for that," I said. "I can't believe Jaz is going to be a model. A real model. They used to call us ugly when we were little kids."

"Well, at least Jasmine grew out of it," Mr. P said. "When are you going to?"

"Man," I said, fanning him off. "Your dad has jokes for days."

"DeMarco," Mr. P said, "I have something I need to talk to you about."

"Okay," I said, fearing the worst.

"School," he said. "I spoke with the people you asked me to talk to and they want you expelled for the remainder of this school year. I'm not sure what they want you to do, but they don't even want you going to the alternative school. It blows my mind that so-called educators will deny a kid his education."

"Well, Mr. P," I said, "I do have a pretty bad rap sheet. I mean, they don't know that I'm ready to move on. They probably just think I'm running the same old story."

"I appreciate you looking at it from their angle, but I still say they are full of it. They would rather have a kid out on the streets doing nothing than to give him another shot," he said.

"I've had like forty-five hundred million shots, Mr. P," I said.

"Well, they need to give you forty-five million and one," he said. "I don't believe in giving up on kids. You can give up on yourself, but I believe it only takes a spark and you never know when that spark will take. And once it takes, the next thing you know you have a wildfire of a kid. You could be the president of the United States."

"Man," I said. "I'll have the White House crunk. We'd be partying up in there all day. I'll have my little secretary of state wearing lil short dresses. I'll hire all strippers to work in the kitchen. Be table dances for everybody."

"Maybe we don't want you to be the president, then," Mr. P said, shaking his head.

"I'll vote for ya, Dee," Blake said and balled up his fist to give me a pound.

"Both of y'all are a little off upstairs," Mr. P said.

The chef placed food on our plates and we laughed and joked with the other people who were seated around our table.

After dinner Mr. P asked me if I wanted to spend the night. I was anxious to see where and how he lived. I had been staying at my grandmother's house since the incident happened with Jaz, and I needed a getaway.

"I would love to, but I was supposed to take my girlfriend to the movies tonight," I said.

"Girlfriend," Blake and Mr. P said at the same time.

"Yes," I said. "What are you two, twins?"

"We were gonna do a little bowling," Blake said.

"Bowling? Man, I don't know how to bowl."

"Neither does my dad, but that never stopped him from getting out there and giving it a shot," Blake said and turned to Mr. P to give him a playful punch to the arm. "Way to hang in there, Dad."

"Get your hands off me, boy. And you're crazy," Mr. P said, pushing his son off him. "I bet you a hundred push-ups that I will get a better score than you."

"Make it easy on yourself, Father," Blake said with a smile.

I was loving this scene and wanted as much of it as possible. This was how I was going to be with my son whenever I had one. Mr. P was now the standard in my eyes. He paid for our food and we left the restaurant. The valet brought the Range Rover around and I got into the backseat.

"So tell me about this girlfriend, Dee," Mr. P said as we pulled out onto Peachtree Street in Buckhead.

"What would you like to know, Mr. P?" I said.

"Is she sane, can she see? I mean, talk to me. What would make a sane woman who has good eyesight want to date a man with a tattoo on his face?"

"She wants me to get rid of the tattoo. So she must not be too sane," I said.

"Oh," Mr. P said. "That changes everything. Get her on the phone and see if she wants to join us. I like her already."

After about fifteen minutes of driving, we pulled up in front of one of the nicest houses I'd ever seen, and that included what I saw on television.

"You live here?" I asked, still gawking at the big, beautiful building that looked more like a library than somebody's house.

"Yessir," Mr. P said. "Welcome to our home, my man."

"And you say you work for a nonprofit?" I asked.

"It's *his* nonprofit, but my mom is an attorney," Blake said with a smile. I could tell he was proud of his mother.

Mr. P pulled into the garage beside a white Range Rover just like the one we were riding in. Once he turned the truck off, I stepped out.

"Is that yours, Blake?"

"I wish," he said. "I don't even have a bicycle. That's my mom's car."

"That's because you left your bicycle in the driveway. You know your mother can't drive."

"Yeah. That's true," Blake said. "My mom crushed my bike, dude."

"I'm sure you'll get another one. I'm sure you get anything you want," I said.

"Nah," he said. "It's not like that around here, brother man. Come on in."

I followed Mr. P and Blake into the house. This place was off the chain. Hardwood floors and marble countertops went on for days. We went into the kitchen where a very pretty lady was standing with her hands on her hips. She had light skin and long, silky hair. She looked like a taller version of Jada Pinkett Smith. "So you couldn't wait for us, huh, Prodigy?" she said to Mr. P.

"DeMarco," he said, "this is my wife, Nina. Where are the girls?"

"They are having a sleepover at Hanna's house. And how are you, baby?" she said, reaching out and shaking my hand and giving me a pleasant smile. "So you are Prodigy's tattoo-faced friend, huh? Well, I like it."

"Thank you," I said. "You're the first adult who likes it."

"It's creative and it sets you apart from everyone else. Who wants to look like everyone else?" she said.

"Not me," I said with a smile.

The more I looked at Mr. P's wife, the more I wanted my own mother to get it together.

"DeMarco is spending the night and we are going to do a little bowling."

"Oh yeah?" she said. "Well, it's nice to have you over, DeMarco."

"Thanks," I said. "I was gonna ask if I could move in."

"Sure," she said. "Come on. I have lots of work that you and Blake can team up on."

I laughed.

"Come on, dude. Let's go down to the basement and shoot some pool."

I walked downstairs with Blake and was amazed at how big this house was. When they said go bowling, I didn't realize they were talking about bowling in their own bowling alley. This was crazy. I turned and checked the place out. They had framed football and basketball jerseys from all kinds of people. They had Kobe, LeBron, D-Wade, Jordan, Michael Vick's Eagle's jersey, Brett Favre, and a few others. I saw a pair of boxing gloves that were sitting in a glass case. They had somebody's signature on them, but I couldn't tell whose.

"Man," I said, "I've never seen anything like this. I don't mean to be riding your jock, but you got it made, man."

"I only live here. I don't pay the bills," he said.

"Yeah, so that's even better. You get to live here for free."

We shared a laugh, then he started racking the pool balls.

Mr. P came down and took the stick from Blake and pushed him away.

Blake chuckled and charged at him. Mr. P dropped the stick and they started wrestling. Blake's mom walked down and picked the stick off the floor, never saying a word to them, and motioned for me to break.

"They don't have the sense God gave a billy goat," she said.

Mr. P had Blake in some kind of leg hold and Blake started yelling that he was tapping out. Mr. P stood up and walked over to his wife. "Now I had to go through all of that to get my stick, and you just gonna come down here and pick it up."

"This is not what you want, Prodigy," she said, lowering the stick and firing a ball into the corner pocket.

"Show off," he said, then walked over and took my stick. He searched around the table for a shot, then seemed to turn serious. "DeMarco."

"Yes," I said.

"I want you to go to this school."

"How? I'm kicked out."

"It's a private school. It's called Jimrose Christian Academy. I can get you in there, but I'm going to need for you to keep everything squeaky clean."

"Where is it?"

"It's out in Gwinnett County," he said.

"How am I gonna get out to Gwinnett County from the Bluff every day?"

"We'll figure all of that out later. I need to know if you want to go or not."

"I'm in," I said. "I'm sure it'll be better than sitting around doing nuttin' in the Bluff all day."

"I agree," Mr. P said.

"Give him that stick back. You suck," Nina said.

Mr. P handed me the stick and smiled as if he was doing what a good husband would do. He winked at me and walked over to take a seat in one of the high-back stools that surrounded the pool table. His wife nodded at me as if to say "you see who runs things in this camp."

I leveled my stick to the table, took a shot, and missed badly. "I guess I'm not used to shooting pool on something this nice."

"No excuses, man," Nina said, then took another shot and pocketed two balls. She placed the stick against the table. "This is too easy. Prodigy, he's more your speed."

"Whatever," he said. "Dee, you get some practice in. I'ma go handle a few things. Call me when you're ready to bowl."

I watched as he and his wife carried on with each other and felt like I was in a good place. I looked around and noticed Blake was sitting on this huge wraparound leather sectional playing video games. The television, if you could call it that, was so big that it covered the entire wall. I pulled out my cell and dialed Morgan's number.

"Hi there," she said. "Where are you?"

"I'm somewhere out in the middle of heaven and earth," I said, looking around at the space I was in.

"Well, why am I not there with you?" she said.

I told her where I was and she said she understood, as long as I promised to make some time for her tomorrow. I also told her about this school that Mr. P said he could get me into.

"Are you serious?" Morgan said excitedly. "That's great. If you can get in there, you'll be doing the doggone thing, Dee."

"Oh yeah," I said. "I don't know anything about private schools."

"School is school, Dee. Just be yourself," she said. "When do you start?"

"I don't know. I gotta go interview or something. I'll keep you posted."

"Okay," she said. "I'm proud of you."

"Thanks. I'm spending the night out here with Mr. P and his family. I'll hook up with you tomorrow, okay?"

"Yeah, that's cool," she said. "Have a good time, and I can't wait to see you. Oh, and Dee?"

"Yeah," I said.

"When you get out to Jimrose, I will kill you if you leave me for one of those white girls," she said.

"Never," I said with a laugh "Not in a million years. It took long enough to make you my boo. Why would I go and mess it up?"

"Good answer," she said before we hung up.

# 17

## JASMINE

I sat in my hospital bed staring out the window. I was tired of lying in the same old bed, eating the same applesauce and Jell-O every day. From what the nurses told me, I had been here for over a week. My side was stitched up and it was hurting like nothing I had ever felt. I had pressed the little button that administered pain medication so many times that they took it from me. All I could think about was getting even with Tiny and Shemika. They were going to pay for doing this to me. I had a punctured lung, and my hand was broken in three places. The nurse told me that if I wouldn't have gotten to the hospital when I did, I would've died. She said if I had arrived three minutes later, I wouldn't be among the living. Thank God for my brother and that driver who Dee credits with saving my life.

I wiggled my hand because it was itching. I tried to sit up a little, but the stitches in my side wouldn't allow me to move much.

There was a knock on my hospital room door and I figured it was Lola, Barry, or DeMarco, but it wasn't any of
them. I did a double take when I saw who it was. Kecia.

My rage returned and I did my best to calm myself.

"Get out," I said. "Get your disloyal, double-crossing
tail out of my room."

"Jaz, wait. Just hear me out," she said. "I didn't have
anything to do with that. The police came and asked me
some questions and I told them everything. Both of them
are locked up."

"And you need to join them," I said.

"Jaz," Kecia said with tears in her eyes. "Why are you so
mad with me? They told me what they were going to do,
and I didn't want nuttin' to do with it. I even called you to
warn you, but I kept getting your voice mail. Check your
messages. I begged you to call me back."

I did see where Kecia was calling me, but I was so livid
at her for leaving me at that party that I wasn't interested
in anything she had to say.

"How did you know where I was?"

"Dee told me. I explained to him how this went down,
and he thanked me for looking out," Kecia said. "I swear
to you that I would never do anything to hurt you, Jaz.
You're my only real friend."

"Yeah, I wish I could say the same thing about you.
Friends who allow their friends to get drugged up. You left
me at a stranger's house."

Kecia started crying and seemed to be hyperventilat-
ing. She walked over and took a seat under the television. I didn't feel anything for her. After what I had
been through, I couldn't care less if she keeled over and
died.

"I-I-I trrried," she said through quick breaths. "I-I tried to get you, but Tiny and Shemika said they had talked to you and you were staying."

"And you believed them? Since when did me and Tiny become so cool that I would pass messages through her?"

"I'm sorry. I'm so sorry, Jaz," Kecia cried.

"Yeah," I said, not interested in her crocodile tears. "You said what you had to say. Now get out."

Kecia looked at me as if her world was about to crumble. As if she couldn't believe I could be so cold. She stood up and gathered herself. She looked at me and mouthed the words *I'm sorry* again before rushing from the room.

No later than two minutes after she left, I had another knock at my door.

"What?" I yelled.

"Why you in here screaming like that?" Sophia said as she walked in looking like she needed to be lying in a bed in the next room over. She had on a yellow sundress that was too big for her and her own hair was sticking out from under a matted wig. She smiled at me as if I was supposed to be happy to see her.

I wasn't.

"How you feeling?" she said as she walked over to my bed.

"I've been better," I said, still seething from Kecia's visit.

"You were wrong for treating that girl like that. You wouldn't want nobody judging you for what somebody else did," Sophia said.

"Why don't you mind your business? You don't even know the whole story," I snapped.

"First of all, you're sixteen. You is my business, and second of all I do know the whole story. She told me when she brought me over here, and I believe her. That girl is a real friend. She ain't had to come in here and subject herself to your lil rant. Did she stab you? Was she their getaway driver? No. She called the police and told them what happened. And she said she gonna testify if it comes to that. You don't find friends like that."

I lay there and listened to my mother. For the first time in years, she sounded like a real mother. And as crazy as it made me feel, I was happy to see her.

"I like your hair like that," she said. "Looks like that pretty girl who that singer boy beat up."

"When did you get out?" I asked.

"I just got out about three or four hours ago. DeMarco bailed me out," she said.

"That was nice of him," I said. "I bet he wished you would've done the same thing for him."

"He ain't like you, Jaz," she said. "That boy don't hold grudges and walk around mad at the world."

"Good for him," I said.

Sophia sighed and shook her head. I know I was a piece of work, but I got it from dealing with her.

"I hope he ain't doing nuttin' illegal that will send his butt where I just came from," she said.

"He's doing tattoos."

"So I hear."

"He is."

"Okay," she said.

I looked away from her and stared out the window. Neither of us said anything for a while. Sophia walked over to the window and stared out too.

"I hear he's going to a private school too. Wonder if his tattoos paying for that?"

"Maybe they are. Why you always gotta jump on the negative side of things?"

"I didn't come up here to fuss with you, chile. If I need to leave, then I will."

"You do whatever you feel like doing," I said.

Sophia smiled and shook her head. "So I hear that you're modeling?" she asked in a small voice.

"I guess," I said.

She nodded her head and appeared on the verge of tears.

"What's wrong with you?" I said and immediately wished I could stop being mean to her.

Sophia shook her head and turned back to the window. As she gazed out at the trees and skyscrapers that were off in the distance, she kept shaking her head, as if she was answering questions in her mind. I looked at my mom and realized that she was a beaten woman, but she was still standing.

"I saw them pictures you took," she said. "Mighty pretty girl you are."

"What pictures?" I asked. "I haven't even seen any pictures that I took."

"Well, I saw 'em," she snapped. "And damn it, you gonna watch your tone with me."

I didn't respond. She was right. Life had been hard for all of us, but she did just get out of jail for shooting a man on my behalf.

"What pictures, and where did you see them?" I said, softening my tone.

"You were wearing some white clothes in one set and some funky feather stuff on the other one. They look nice," she said. "Who would ever think that my baby would be a supermodel?"

"Oh," I said. "So now I'm your baby?"

Sophia turned around and looked at me. "Am I perfect? No! Am I a saint? No! Am I an alcoholic who probably should've never brought a kid into this world, never mind four of 'em? Yes. But let me tell you one thing, little super-model with the attitude from hell. I love all of y'all."

I don't know what it was about hearing her say she loved me, but all of a sudden I started tearing up. I realized that I never recalled her saying those words. I couldn't stop crying, and when I looked at my mother she was crying too.

"Stop that," she said, even though she couldn't stop her own tears from streaming down her bony face. She walked over to the bed and started wiping my tears away. "You just stop that right now."

"Ouch," I said, jerking my head back. "You poked in my eye."

"Oops. I'm sorry," she said, then started laughing.

I used my good hand to rub my eye, then I started laughing with her. She sat on the bed and leaned down and gave me a hug. I hadn't hugged my mother in at least five or six years. I could still smell the alcohol in her skin, but I wasn't interested in her smell, only her touch.

"You know I gotta go to court for shooting Otis? I'm sorry I didn't listen to you, Jaz," she said.

"That's all right," I said. "You got caught up."

"I'll tell you what," she said. "When I saw him looking at that doggone video on the phone, I caught his butt up with some bullets. I know I shouldn't say this, but I wish I would've killed him."

"No," I said. "Then you wouldn't be here."

"You think your big-money friends can get me a good lawyer?"

"If they want me to take another picture, they will," I said. "And if you promise to check yourself into a rehab place."

"Now wait a minute," she said, sitting up.

"It's not up for debate," I said, playing the role of the caregiver. "If you want to stay free, then promise to get yourself cleaned up."

Sophia smiled and showed her raggedy teeth as if she had a dental plan, and shook her head. "What am I gonna do with you, girl?"

"Love me or leave me alone," I said with a smile.

"I think I'll love you," she said and buried her face into the side of my neck. It felt good to be loved.

# 18

# DeMarco

Jimrose Christian Academy was huge. Two hundred acres of well-manicured lawns and well-kept buildings. I had never seen anything like it. As we pulled into the entrance of the school, which was between two waterfalls, I noticed a statue of a man and a woman.

"Who are those people?" I asked Mr. P.

"Those are the founders of the school. His name is Jim and her name is Rose. They were jumped on this education back in the early nineteen hundreds in South Carolina. This started out as a charter school for African Americans, but the founders couldn't bring themselves to exclude anyone, so they opened the doors to everyone. You'll get the rundown on them later, I'm sure."

"Really. Seems like mostly white folks now," I said as I looked around the campus.

"Sad, huh?" he said, shaking his head. "African Americans can come here for little or no money, but for whatever reason we don't take advantage of this."

"Well, it's way out here in the boondocks. I would have to leave home at five in the morning to get here on MARTA."

"They have buses," he said. "You'll get a schedule for that today as well. So don't forget."

"Good morning, Mr. Banks," said an old white man with a thick mustache. He had a quick smile and he leaned over to speak to me. "Good morning, young man."

"Good morning," I replied.

Mr. P pulled away from the guard center and we zigzagged our way through the school grounds.

"You have a quick interview, but it's just a formality, then the basketball coach wants to see you," he said as he pulled into a parking lot. "I'm going to leave you on your own after the interview. I have some other things to take care of. The coach is a real cool guy. His name is Coach Backus. He'll come get you and take care of you from there."

"Okay," I said, looking around at all the kids who were dressed the same. All the boys wore khaki pants and navy-blue shirts. The girls wore khaki skirts and baby-blue shirts. I would be the only guy here in Levi's jeans, Air Max shoes, and an Aéropostale shirt. I continued to gawk at my new school and saw a few small kids who couldn't have been older than kindergarten age. "They have an elementary school here too?"

"Yeah," Mr. P said as we stepped out of his truck. "This place goes from pre-K all the way up to grade twelve. And they have a one hundred percent college rate."

"One hundred percent?"

"Yep," he said. "Let's make sure you don't drop it down to ninety-nine point something. Comprende?"

"I got you," I said. "Now I see why you put that makeup on me to cover my tattoo. I would feel real out of place over here with that on my face."

"Nina knows this guy who can remove it," Mr. P said with a smile.

"Nah," I said. "I like it. We'll keep it covered for now though."

As we walked, I saw this big building with a domed top and a sign above the door that read THE AQUATIC CENTER.

"What is that?"

"The swimming pool," Mr. P said. "They have every sport you can imagine here. Basketball, football, baseball, lacrosse, soccer, volleyball, and any other sport you can think of. They even have a golf team. I hear they are pretty good."

I saw a guy walk by and he looked familiar, but I dismissed the thought because if they had a 100 percent college-bound rate, I was 100 percent sure none of these folks had ever walked in my shoes or hung around the areas that I frequented.

We walked into this building and headed straight to the school store. It wasn't like any school store I had ever seen. The place was about the size of a super Foot Locker. Mr. P motioned for me to follow him to the back. He pointed out the khaki pants and shirts. "Get your size and get changed."

I never wanted to go to a school that required uniforms. I remember when Dr. Rogers tried that at James Charles High and nobody followed the dress code. Parents were up at the school cussing and carrying on, so she just said forget it.

I grabbed the clothes and went into the dressing room.

I quickly changed and folded my clothes up into a neat little bundle.

"Now you look like you're ready for school," he said with a proud smile on his face. "Get four more pair of pants, four more shirts, and come on."

We walked up to the register and Mr. P had already picked out a navy-blue book bag with the Jimrose emblem on it. He had tablets, pens, pencils, a Texas Instruments calculator, and a host of other school supplies. The girl behind the counter, who looked like she was a student herself, rang up all the items and I couldn't believe how much this crap had cost. Five hundred and forty-four dollars.

"Man," I said, looking at Mr. P like he was crazy for paying this much money.

"Don't sweat it," he said. "Just get all As and we'll call it even."

"So is this the young man that you speak so highly of?" said a tall, brown-skinned man who wore a navy-blue warm-up suit with a gold stripe down the side. He walked up to me and extended his hand. "Coach Backus. And you must be DeMarco."

"Yes, sir," I said, shaking the tall man's hand. He had to be at least six-feet-eight-inches tall.

"Welcome to Jimrose," he said with a smile.

"What's good with ya," Mr. P said to Coach Backus, and the two shared a frat-brother-like hug. "Grab the book bag, DeMarco, and I'll take this other stuff home for you."

We walked out of the store and the pretty little white girl who was working the register smiled at me. I looked back at her when we passed the window of the store and she was still looking at me. She waved her hand and I took that as a sign that she liked what she saw. I made a mental note to come back by and see her.

*Uh oh, Morgan*, I thought and kept walking.

"So," Coach Backus said, "Prodigy tells me great things about you. He said you were a high-character guy. Is he pulling my chain?"

"I hope not," I said with a laugh.

"Coach," Prodigy said, looking down at his expensive watch. "I need to run. Will you make sure he gets to his interview?"

"We're skipping the interview. He's good as far as admissions go. I'ma take him over to the gym and see what he can do with a ball."

"Already?" Mr. P asked. "Let the boy go to class before you get him all sweaty."

"Basketball is paying his fifteen-thousand-dollar tuition, so I wanna see what we are getting for our money," he said as if he was a kid with a new toy.

"Whatever, man. The boy is from the hood. You know he has game," Mr. P said.

"No," Coach Backus said. "I've been fooled by that one before. Fool me once, shame on you; but fool me twice, shame on me."

Mr. P shook his head and reached out to shake my hand. "You handle your business up here, DeMarco. Don't embarrass yourself or me. You got me?"

"I got you," I said.

"Take notes in all of your classes and ask your teachers if you can sit up front," he said.

"I will."

"And one more thing," he said, shaking his head. "I'm

proud of you, boy. Two weeks ago this time you were sitting in a cell. Now look at you."

"Thanks to you," I said.

"No," he said. "You did this. This is all on you, son."

"Okay," Coach Backus said. "Let's cut the lovefest short. We need to get to the gym before my class gets there."

Mr. P shook my hand again and did the frat-brother-like thing again with Coach Backus. He looked at his watch again and hustled out of the building.

"Let's head out this way," Coach Backus said as we walked out a side door. We entered another building and I almost couldn't believe what I was seeing. The gym looked like someplace where a college team would play. They had two levels of bleachers that surrounded the court. Someone was running on the track on the second level.

"Man," I said. "This place is crazy."

"It's pretty nice. Sit tight for a minute. I'll be right back," he said and walked across the gym floor and into a glassed-in office.

I took a seat on the first-level bleachers and took in the scenery.

"What's upper, Mr. New Guy," a boy with orange hair and freckles on his face said as he walked in the door of the gym. He was loud and I could tell right away that he was used to getting his way.

I looked at the guy and smiled. He reminded me of a white Will Smith in *The Fresh Prince of Bel-Air*. He had on a pair of Timberland boots and they were unlaced. His navy-blue blazer was turned inside out, his shirt wasn't tucked in, and his pants were hanging down below his waistline.

"Kyle Whiteside is the name," he said and reached out to me with a closed fist.

I tapped fist with him. "DeMarco Winslow."

"How are you, Mr. Winslow? I might as well let you know right now that I'm the best player on the basketball team, the football team, and the tennis team. I would be the best player on the baseball team if I had time to play."

"Sounds like you're a stud," I said sarcastically.

"You been talking to one of these hoochies around here?" he said, then burst out laughing at himself. "Coach B Diddy asked me to come in here and check you out. I guess he thinks you're some kind of competition or something, but what the fool fails to realize is that there is no competition. I always find a way to win. Always."

"Is that right," I said and knew right away that I was going to have some problems at Jimrose Christian Academy.

"Yeah, that's right. And I'll do you in my Timbos, boy."

I laughed because Kyle Whiteside was funny.

Coach Backus came out of his office with a basketball. He tossed it to me, but Kyle snatched it and started dribbling toward the basket. He made a layup, got his rebound, and dribbled out to the three-point line and shot a jumper. It went straight through the rim, touching only the nets.

He looked at me and shook his head.

"I just wanna see your form," Coach Backus said to me.

I walked out on the court and Kyle threw me the ball.

"Let's see whatcha got, big-timer," he said.

I dribbled the ball a few times, then pulled up a jumper that clanked off the backboard, and I wasn't sure the ball even hit the rim.

Coach Backus rebounded the ball and threw it back to me. I shot again and got about the same results.

"Nice," he said, nodding his head. "I like that."

"Yeah," Kyle said. "We can use another brick mason, Coach. That's just what we need."

"Go to class, Kyle. Why are you in here, anyway?"

"I came to check out the new booty. Looks like I wasted my time. He sucks like the other three black guys you went out and got to try to save the day," he said, then walked over to the bleachers, picked up his bag, and threw up the peace sign.

"Never mind that boy," Coach said. "His daddy has like a gazillion dollars, so he feels he can do whatever he wants whenever he wants. That mouth of his is going to get him into some big trouble one of these days."

"He has a nice shot," I said, giving the loudmouth his proper due.

"Not really," Coach Backus said. "He's a set shooter. I see that you take your shot off of the dribble. Kyle has to stand still. What defense worth its salt is gonna wait for you to get set?"

"Not many," I said. "I haven't played ball in months. I'll get back into the swing of things after a few days of playing."

"Oh yeah," Coach said. "Can you touch the rim?"

I dribbled the ball down the center of the lane, planted my feet, and exploded off the floor and shot up above the rim. I pumped the ball, then dunked it hard with both hands.

Coach smiled and nodded his head.

"Yeah," I said. "I can touch it."

"I would say so," he said. "Let me show you to your classes. I think we have a keeper."

Coach showed me to all my classes, then we walked back to the one I was supposed to be in now. "I'll have your stuff at practice today. We start at four thirty on the dot, but I'm going to need for you to get there a little early today. I need to get you a locker and a few other things."

"Okay, Coach," I said. "I'll come over right after my last class."

"Good," he said, then walked down the hallway.

I walked into my math classroom and took a seat. The teacher was this older white lady and she nodded her head at an open chair. She seemed pleasant, but I guessed I would see. She stood and walked over to me and handed me today's assignment. Everything on the paper looked like gibberish. It might as well have been Chinese because I was totally lost.

"I've seen that look before," Kyle Whiteside said. "It says, what the hell you talking about, Willis?"

Nobody laughed, even though I thought what he said was hilarious.

The teacher stood and walked over to me. She pulled a chair up and took a seat. "Hi," she said in a quiet and soothing tone. "I'm Mrs. Free. Welcome to Jimrose. Do you understand this assignment?"

"No, ma'am," I said.

"Well, let's get you up to speed," she said.

After a five-minute tutorial session, I had a good grasp on what to do. I completed all the questions and handed them to her right after the bell sounded.

"Just a second, DeMarco," she said, going over the classwork.

I stood by her desk as she went over the paper with a red-ink pen. She put a mark on every single one of the problems.

"This is pretty good," she said, then wrote an eighty on the top of the paper. "Not bad, but I want you to take this home and study it. If you bring it in corrected, I will give you credit for it."

"Look at cha," Kyle said. "Giving out charity already, but I guess you're used to that, huh, homeboy?"

I wanted to break Kyle's face, but I didn't even respond to him.

"I'll give you another hundred for ignoring him," she said with a smile. "Have a good day, DeMarco."

I walked out into the hallways, which were packed with kids.

I saw the guy who I thought looked familiar and I walked over to him. "Where do I know you from?" I said.

He looked at me and his face broke out into a wide smile.

"Jail," he said. "It's me, Franky. I'm from New Orleans."

"What's up, roomie," I said and reached out to give him a brotherly hug. Franky was a guy who came to Metro one time and one time only. Some guy had beat up his girlfriend so he got himself arrested just so he could beat up the perpetrator. He was cool, and I gave him his first tattoo right in our cell.

"Whatchu doing here?" he asked.

"You remember Mr. P?" I asked. "He let you use his cell phone to call your people."

"Yeah," Franky said. "Of course I remember him. He did the book club thing for you guys, right?"

"Yep," I said. "Well, I got kicked out of my other school, so he got me in here."

"That's what's up," Franky said, still smiling. He pulled up the sleeve of his shirt. "Remember this?"

I looked down at the tattoo of a New Orleans Saints emblem and smiled. "How could I forget my own work?"

"Yeah," he said. "How do you like it up here so far?"

"I just got here, but it seems cool," I said. "Well, with the exception of this clown named Kyle Whiteside. Do you know him?"

"Who doesn't? Just ignore him, bro. He's not worth you getting kicked out. Because it will be you that gets kicked out; he's not going anywhere. They make new rules for him. I think his dad gives the school like two or three million dollars every year, so he's good. He has a sister that goes here too. She's cool, dates a brother and everything."

"And their pops don't have a problem with that?"

"Not that I know of," he said. "Seems like everyone in the family is cool except freckle face."

"You playing on the basketball team?"

"Nah," Franky said. "I play football. Our coach is over the top. By the time the season is over, I need a break."

"Man," I said, "I was hoping I would have someone to keep me off of that fool, Kyle. I don't know how long I'm going to be able to keep ignoring that fool."

Franky fanned away my concerns. "He's like a stray cat. He's always looking for attention. If you give it to him, he'll keep coming around. If you ignore him, he'll move on. Listen. I gotta get to class, bro, but I'll holla at you at lunch. What time do you go?"

I pulled out my schedule and scanned it. Franky looked

down at it and sucked his tooth. "Dag. We're on different zones, but I'll switch it up today. I'll find you."

"Cool," I said and shook hands with him again.

It felt good to have a friend at this new place. I walked to class and sat down in the front. The teacher was a short black man with thick glasses.

"Welcome to American History. Most of what we will learn is a lie, but they pay me to teach it so that's what I'll do," he said.

I looked at the short guy and smiled.

Yeah, I was beginning to think I was going to like Jimrose Christian Academy.

# 19

## JASMINE

I was out of the hospital and resting comfortably in my own bed. Not my bed at Barry's house, or the one over in the Bluff, but my own bed in my own condominium. Technically it belonged to Sophia, since I was still a minor, but I was paying the bills. We had a four-bedroom, fully furnished pad with flat-screen televisions in almost every room. I had the master suite—even though I tried to give it to Sophia, she knew how to shut me up.

"Girl," she said when we moved in, "if I sleep in this room every night, I'ma need a few glasses of wine just to stop myself from having a heart attack."

Needless to say, she got the smallest room in the condo.

I wasn't really digging living all the way out in Gwinnett County, but since this was the only place my brother could go to school, we decided that this was the only place for us. It was almost like old times with the four of us together.

My tutor had just left and I was free for the rest of the

day. No photo shoots or anything. I wasn't completely healed up, but I was getting there. It had been five weeks since my attack and I had just gotten my cast off. My doctors suggested that I get out and walk for a mile or so every day, and DeMarco wanted me to have some company so he bought me a teacup Yorkie, Mr. Snuggles.

"I'ma tell your lil black butt one more time and then I'ma flush you down the toilet," Sophia said.

I laughed. Mr. Snuggles must've made a boo-boo on the floor again. He was only six weeks old—what did she expect?

"Devin," I said to my little brother, "you wanna go out for a walk?"

"No," he said from his favorite spot on the floor in front of the television. He was watching some kids' show with a bunch of cartoon characters.

"I'm going out for a walk. I'll be right back," I said and put Mr. Snuggles on his leash.

We walked out the door and around the complex. I loved coming outside. The yards were always so neat and clean. The neighbors were all nice people and everything was perfect. Strangers couldn't just pop up, because there was a big guard out front and the condos were surrounded by a six-foot-tall gate. So why was I staring at somebody who I knew I didn't let in.

"Hey, Jaz," Kecia said.

"Kecia," I said. "How did you get in here?"

"Girl," she said, "just because you living high on the hog don't act like you ain't from the Bluff. You know we make a way when we want something."

"So what do you want?" I asked.

"I want us to be friends again," she said.

"We're straight, and I'm sorry for snapping on you like I did. I thought since Tiny and Shemika were your rolling partners that you were in on it."

"I would never do anything to hurt you. You were my friend when nobody else was. You stood by me when people used to throw bottles at me and call me ugly. When I wanted to kill myself, you were the one who talked me out of it and made me feel like I was worth something. So let me tell you something: I'm not walking away from a friend like you. You're gonna have to do a lot more than ignore my calls and cuss me out."

"I said we're straight," I said, feeling a little bit of nostalgia.

"That's an ugly dog, Jaz," she said.

"You're crazy," I said, leaning down and scooping up Mr. Snuggles. I rubbed noses with my little pet. "Tell her you're sexy."

"I'm just playing," she said. "He's cute."

"I know," I said.

"You know Tiny and Shemika took a plea, don't you?"

"No, I didn't," I said. "What did they get?"

"Ten years. They tried to testify against each other and everything. There is truly no honor among thieves. I testified against both of them—now I hear they are in jail plotting against each other."

"Well, I wish them well in their self-destruction," I said.

"Jolly got shot last night," she said. "They say he gonna live though."

"You know what, Kecia," I said. "I can't do this. We are cool and we can hang, but I can't do the ghetto gossip. I didn't do it when I lived over there, and I'm not going to do it now. I wanna leave that Bluff life right in the Bluff."

Kecia nodded her head.

"How did you know where I was living?"

"Your mom," Kecia said.

"I'm about to put her out. If she tells one more person where I live . . ."

"I'm proud of Miss Sophia," Kecia said. "She's gaining weight and looking good."

"She eats twenty-four-seven."

My cell phone rang and the screen said Lola.

"Hello," I said.

"I have great news," she said. Every time she called me she said the same thing.

"I'm all ears," I said.

"You're going to Paris. Katina Elon wants to shoot you for an exclusive line of women's dresses."

"When?"

"Tonight. You'll be gone for four weeks."

"Okay," I said. "Wait. I can only do three. My mom's court date is coming up. I need to be there."

"Okay," Lola said. "I don't think that'll be a problem."

"Good," I said.

"Don't sound so excited. This is huge."

"I hope there is a huge paycheck attached to it," I said.

"Bigger than anything I've ever gotten, and, girl, I'm prettier than you," Lola said.

I laughed and said my good-byes.

"I gotta go to Paris tonight," I said.

Kecia's eyes lit up. "Are you serious? Oh my God. You're like a model for real for real? Like you're about to be on magazine covers and stuff?"

"Yeah," I said with a sigh.

I wasn't really feeling this modeling life, but it was better than living in the Bluff.

"I wish I could go to Paris," she said.

I turned my phone around and dialed Lola back.

"Good evening, darling," she said in her faux French accent.

"I need a ticket for my friend. She wants to go with me."

"Is your friend of age?"

"She's seventeen."

"Text message me her info and I'll get her name on the manifest. We don't do tickets, darling. We only fly private."

"What is that?"

"You'll see," she said, then hung up the phone.

"Okay," I said to Kecia. "Be ready at six o'clock. We'll have a car come pick you up. And don't tell anyone about this. I don't need anybody tryna kidnap me."

Kecia stood there with a blank look on her face. Tears welled up in her eyes and she ran over to me. She hugged my neck so hard I started to punch her.

"I love you, girl," she said.

"I love you too, Kecia. Now go get ready."

# 20

# DeMarco

We were one hour away from our first game. B.o.B played over the speakers in the locker room and all the players seemed ready to go. I walked over to the mirror and checked myself out. I felt good in my white fitted jersey and oversize shorts. I was given number four. I didn't like it and I asked for number one, but Kyle being the buttwipe that he was, claimed he wanted it. Even though for the last two years he wore number ten.

*What a jerk,* I thought.

Speaking of Kyle, where was he? I looked around and didn't see his face nor did I hear his loud mouth.

"Yo, Danny. Have you seen Kyle?" I asked our power forward.

"Nah," he said.

"Kevin," I said to our backup point guard. He was the starter until I showed up. "Have you seen Kyle?"

"Sure haven't, Dee. He was in class today, but I haven't seen him since," he said.

"Has anybody seen Kyle?" I yelled over the music.

Everyone shook their heads. I didn't like the clown one bit, but he was good and we needed him. Once I got back into the swing of things and found my shooting touch, I quickly became the best basketball player on the team, and he didn't like that one bit. He even took a swing at me after practice one day. I ducked out of his way and his own momentum caused him to fall. I walked over and offered him a hand to help him up.

He took my hand, thanked me, then told me he was gonna kick my black butt one day.

"Coach," I said, walking into the big man's office, "Kyle is a no-show."

Coach Backus stopped what he was doing and looked up from his desk at me. "What do you mean, he's a no-show? He was in class today."

"I know, but he's not here now."

"Got dog it," Coach said, standing and walking out into the locker room. Once he didn't see Kyle he turned the music down.

"Who has his cell phone number?" Coach Backus asked all of the guys.

"Nobody talks to Kyle unless we have to. Who would want his cell phone number?" Mitchell, our skinny Asian trainer, said.

"I got his sister's number," Buzz Lightyear, our seven-feet-tall center, said.

"Call her," Coach snapped.

Buzz Lightyear's real name was Manny Banionis. He was only sixteen years old and already had a full beard. He was from Lithuania and spoke with a thick accent. His hair was always cut close to his head, so everyone called him Buzz Lightyear. Buzz dialed the number and started talking to whoever answered the phone.

Everyone had a hard time making out what he was saying, so Coach Backus snatched the phone from him.

"Monday morning," he said to Buzz with a pointed finger, "you take your butt to the office and get an English support class."

"I speak language good English, good Coach," Buzz said with a wide smile.

"Hi," Coach said into the phone and acted as if he wanted to punch Buzz. "How you doing? This is Coach Backus. Is Kyle at home? Wait a minute. Calm down. Where is your father? Will you have him call me as soon as he gets in, please?"

Coach hung up the phone with a distressed look on his face.

"You a'ight, Coach?" I asked.

"That fool stole some money from his mom and took her car."

"He did what?"

"Yes," Coach said. "The sister said their mom is worried sick over him. I'll go over there after the game. That's if he doesn't show up."

"You want me to go with you, Coach?"

"You can if you want to," he said. "Let's go in here and warm up."

Jimrose easily dominated our opponents. I had forty-three points, fourteen rebounds, and seven assists. I would've filled up the stat sheet even more, but Coach Backus pulled me out of the game because I took an elbow to the face and I hit the floor. Coach ran out on the floor and placed a towel over my face. I wasn't even hurt. It wasn't even that bad of a shot, but he acted like I was knocked unconscious. He helped me up and rushed me to the locker room. I was new at the school and didn't want to make any waves, so I went along with him.

"Coach," I said. "What's the problem? I'm all right."

"Cover that thing up, boy," he said, pointing at my tattoo.

I looked in the mirror and saw the bottom half of my tattoo showing.

"Those boosters out there are screaming your name now, but if they see that," he said, jabbing a finger at my face, "they will turn on you like a snake."

"Why?"

"Why?" he asked me. "What do you mean, why? Because nobody likes thugs but other thugs. And we have a good school here and nobody wants a thug to come and ruin it. People don't want their kids around thugs and real students don't have time to be around them either. They're like roaches. Once one comes a whole lot more will follow."

"I hear everything you say, Coach," I said, getting pissed off that he was judging me. "I've been here for almost two months and you've never heard one bad thing about me. All my grades are up and I get along with everybody, so why are you calling me a thug? I'm not a thug."

"That's true. I know that, you know that, but they don't know that," he said, jerking his hand toward the people out in the gym. "Your appearance is all people who don't know you have to go on. So put some more makeup on that thing and come back out."

"A'ight," I said.

"Hey, man," Coach Backus said. "You're a great kid, De-Marco, and you played a heckuva game tonight. Hurry up and come back out and watch the applause you get."

I smiled and walked over to my locker. I opened it up and removed the Dermablend makeup that had become part of my daily life at Jimrose. I applied a little of it to my face and put the top back on it. I closed my locker and was about to walk back out when I heard someone banging on the door. I walked over and opened it. It was the white girl from the student store. I'd seen her around the campus, but I never got a chance to talk to her. Now wasn't a good time for her to try to talk to me because Morgan was out in the stands.

She walked inside and didn't seem like she was there to flirt.

"You're DeMarco, right?" she said and wiped her eyes.

"Yes," I said. "What's wrong?"

"I'm Tabitha," she said as if that was supposed to mean something to me. "Kyle's sister. He's in trouble."

"What kind of trouble is Kyle in?"

"Big trouble," she said. "He owes some guys some money and my dad isn't giving him anything. Kyle wants to be a thug, but he's really a nice guy."

I had been around the guy long enough to know that he was far from a nice guy.

"What's going on?" I asked. "How can I help you?"

"He's being held by this gang in the hood somewhere. They say he owes them twenty thousand dollars. My mom can't access that kind of cash and my dad just flat out said no."

"I don't have that kind of money," I said. "What hood is he in?"

"I don't—" she said but was interrupted by her cell phone.

Tabitha answered the phone, then handed it to me.

"What's up, Kyle?"

"Who is this?"

"DeMarco," I said. "Where are you?"

"What are you doing at my house? You better not be having sex with my sister. I know she has jungle fever and all, but damn."

"Man," I said, "I'm not at your house. I'm at school. The same place you would be if you weren't out trying to play superthug. Now where are you?"

"I need some money, dude. I'm sure you don't have the kind of money I need, so I don't know why she put you on the phone."

"Kyle," I snapped, "shut up and tell me where you at."

"You need to learn how to speak proper English, dude," he said, and I thought I heard his words slur.

"Are you drunk or high?"

"No," he said. "What I am is tied up. I need some money for these fools."

"What fools?"

"These Vine City Hustler fools."

"Wow," I said. "Whisper the names of the people you're with?"

Kyle spoke in a low voice and I recognized one of the names.

"Sit tight," I said. "Not that you have much of a choice. I'll see what I can do."

I ended the call with Kyle and punched my number into Tabitha's phone. "I need to get back out here and you need to get out of this locker room. Text message me his number. I just put mine in your phone. I'll see what I can do."

I walked back out into the gym and everyone stood on their feet and started clapping. I waved to the crowd.

"Looks king brand-new town," Buzz said with his trademark bright smile. He gave me a high five.

"What?" I said.

"He said it looks like a brand-new king is in town," Danny, the forward, said.

I shook my head and rushed over to give my friend Morgan a hug. Between her busy schedule and me living out in the boondocks, we barely had time to see each other. We decided that it was best that we stay friends and nothing more. We both agreed that if our thing was meant to be, then love would find a way to make it happen.

"You played great, boy."

"Thank ya," I said. "Lack of competition will make you look better than you really are."

"I don't know. Those white boys could shoot. They were draining threes like they were layups."

"They were pretty good," I said. "Listen. I need to ride back over to the Bluff with you. One of the dudes on the team is caught up with some Vine City dudes. I'ma go see if I can help him out."

"I thought you had problems with them too," she said.

"Nah," I lied. "We squashed that."

"Oh good," she said. "Well, I'll be right here waiting on you."

"Thanks," I said, then walked back into the locker room to get changed.

# 21

## DEMARCO

Morgan and I talked about how much things had changed with me and Jasmine over the last month or so. She was off taking pictures in Paris and I was running around at a school that cost fifteen thousand dollars a year. I asked her to try to come out to Jimrose, but she had laid her roots down at James Charles High and wasn't trying to leave. She dropped me off at Jolly's house and we said our good-byes.

I walked up the steps to Jolly's front porch and rang his doorbell. I heard something to my left and I turned my head just in time to see his mother squatting down by the side of the house. She was urinating. I frowned and shook my head.

"Whatchu want dere on my porch, boy," she said, not bothering to stop.

"I'm looking for Jolly," I said. "Why you out here using the bathroom when you got one in the house?"

"Why you minding my business?"

"My bad."

"Jolly ain't here, but if you give me five dollars I'll tell you where he is," she said.

I walked back down the steps and over to where she was standing. I reached in my pocket and handed her a five-dollar bill. Just then the front door swung open and Jolly stood on the other side.

"There he go," his mother said, pointing toward the front door.

I reached out for my money and she jerked her hand back with the quickness of a cat. Crackheads and cats are the quickest species known to man. I smiled at her but she didn't smile back. She took off walking down the street in search of her next high.

"Player," Jolly said, "what's good with ya?"

I handed him a wad of money as repayment for the money he loaned me to get my mother bailed out. He took it, didn't bother to count it, and stuck it in his pocket.

"What's good with ya, family," I said as I ran back up the steps and walked into Jolly's house. The place was humid and hot. I was getting spoiled living out with the wealthy folks.

We did our brotherly hug thing, then I got down to business.

"I got this white boy who plays on my team, right?"

"Right."

"He's over here somewhere. His mom and sister are worried sick about him. I know who got him, but I can't get into it with them Vine City fools, man. I got a good thing going out there in Gwinnett County."

"Who got him?" Jolly asked.

"Dominique and his cronies," I said.

"Is tonight my lucky night or what?" Jolly said. "That's the fool that shot me."

Jolly walked over to his closet and pulled out a gun. My heart skipped a beat. Here I was, back in the heat of battle again. I did not want to go back to jail, and if I walked out that door with Jolly, there was a very good chance that's where I would be headed.

"Come on," Jolly said.

I paused for a second or two, then followed him out of the house. As we walked down the street, my cell phone vibrated. I looked at the screen and it was a private number. I answered.

"They gonna kill me if you don't bring the money," Kyle screamed. There was sheer panic and fear in his voice. Then the phone went dead.

"They got ole boy shook," I said to Jolly. "That was him screaming on the phone that they gonna kill him."

"This dude must be pretty cool with ya," Jolly said as we ran across Joseph E. Boone Boulevard.

"Not at all," I said. "I don't like him one bit, but I still don't want him to die. I like his sister. She's good people and she loves his sorry butt, so that's why I'm here."

"You out there hitting the white girls, Dee?"

We walked along a path and Jolly held up his hand for me to be quiet. We eased up on this house as we saw two guys on the back porch. One of them was Kyle and he didn't appear to be tied up or in any kind of danger. As a matter of fact, he seemed to be enjoying himself very much. He and Dominique were wrapped in a lip-lock and appeared to be tongue wrestling. Dominique turned Kyle around and was kissing on his neck.

I had no idea that Dominique or Kyle were gay. A tall, skinny wannabe gangster. Jolly lifted his pistol and walked toward them. "Well hello, ladies," Jolly said.

"Man!" The skinny guy jumped back, holding his heart. He held out his hands to Jolly and started begging. "I'm sorry, Jolly. My gun slipped. I didn't mean to shoot you, man. I swear I didn't."

I came out of the shadows and looked at Kyle. When he saw me his eyes became wide and he knew he was busted.

"Come here," I barked.

He walked over to me and dropped his head. I reached up and slapped him hard. His stringy red hair went every which way.

"Get your ass in your car," I said.

He held his head where I slapped him and walked around to the front of the house without a word. I told Jolly that I would holla at him later and I jumped in the passenger seat of Kyle's mom's car. Now that Dominique's secret was out, he would no longer be a problem for anybody. Jolly had a big mouth.

"Please don't tell anybody, DeMarco. I'll pay you whatever you ask. Just please don't tell anybody."

"I don't care anything about your sexuality, dude," I said. "I just don't appreciate you playing games with your family like that. You're lucky to have a family who cares about you."

"I know, but promise me you won't tell anybody."

"I'm not promising you jack, homie."

I didn't speak anymore for the entire ride back to Gwinnett County, even though Kyle babbled on and on about how he was sorry and how Dominique made him do this. He begged me not to tell his parents about his little charade. I sat there and listened but didn't say anything either way. We pulled up at Kyle's house and it was even bigger and nicer than Mr. P's. His father was waiting outside when we pulled into the driveway.

Kyle parked, got out of the car, and ran past his dad. He went into the house and his mother met him at the door. She was crying and reached out to hug what she thought was her newly freed son.

"Mr. Winslow," the rich man said. Mr. Whiteside owned two professional sports teams already and was making a bid for the Atlanta Falcons. He was filthy rich. "Thank you."

"No problem," I said and debated whether I was going to tell Kyle's secret or not. I decided that I would keep it for him. Maybe that would keep his mouth from running so much. "Now I need a favor from you."

"What's that?"

"I need a ride home," I said.

"Do you have a driver's license?" he asked.

"No sir."

"Can you drive?" he asked.

"Yes, sir," I said.

"You can take Kyle's car. Take my card. If you get stopped, have the officer call me. What is that on your face, son? I didn't see that at the game tonight."

"It's a tattoo, but I have to cover it up when I'm at school."

"Why?"

"My people think it will turn people off," I said. "They don't want folks thinking I'm a thug."

"You're all right with me, and I'm the biggest booster that school's ever had. I want you to stop with the makeup. You're not a girl. Be yourself, and if anyone says anything to you, tell them to call me."

"A'ight," I said with a smile. "My kind of guy."

He handed me the keys to a yellow Corvette.

"Kyle won't be needing that for a while, so have fun. I think I'm going to send his butt to military school. The registration and everything you need is in the glove compartment."

I walked over to the shiny sports car and smiled.

"I don't want to get in any trouble, Mr. Whiteside. I appreciate the offer, but I can't drive without a license."

"Tabby!" he called.

His daughter ran outside. "Yes, Daddy," she said.

"Give DeMarco here a ride home," the rich man said. "Once you get that driver's license, you come back over here and get your car."

"Will do," I said. "Will do."

# Epilogue

## DeMarco

We were playing in the championship game and the place was packed. Kyle's dad had a change of heart and allowed him to stay at Jimrose. He was a totally different guy now that he knew I knew his secret. We were down by two with fifteen seconds on the clock. I had the ball at the top of the key. I saw the double-team coming but waited until they had fully committed. At the last second I flung a chest pass to Kyle. He set his feet and let one fly.

*Swish.*

The bottom of the net was the only thing that moved.

The buzzer sounded and we were officially Region 5 AAA champs.

My sister ran out onto the court followed by my mother, who was freshly acquitted of all charges stemming from her shooting incident. They hugged me like we had won the NBA finals. Mrs. Eichelberger and her husband were up clapping and giving me the thumbs-up sign.

Devin was locked onto Mrs. Eichelberger's leg and didn't know what was going on. Mr. P and his wife were doing some dance in celebration of our victory. Blake stayed home and watched his sisters. He said we were going to lose anyway.

*Ha-haaaa. Take that, sucker.*

After twenty minutes or so, everything had settled down. The entire team was standing on the podium, preparing to accept our trophies, when the lights went out.

A voice came across the speaker system.

*Stop what you're doing. Stop what you're doing. We have a special championship performance by none other than . . . the Microphone Master, Moochieeeee!*

"Get ya hands up. Everybody in the house get ya hands up," Uncle Moochie barked as he paced back and forth in his all-white Adidas warm-up suit, white shell-toe Adidas shoes, and matching Kangol hat.

"If ya wanna hear the Microphone Master, Moochie, let me hear you say, oh yeahhhhh."

And the crowd screamed all at once.

*Oh yeahhhhh!*

He was finally getting a chance to perform. I couldn't do anything but smile and scream, "Oh yeah."

# In Stores Now!

### *Two the Hard Way*

Romeo is seventeen and the star quarterback for the Tucker Tigers. He gets all the attention he can handle from the honeys—and the big-time college football programs. Deciding where to take a scholarship should be Romeo's biggest problem, but these days it's the last thing on his mind . . .

Not only is Kwame finally getting out of jail, their absentee mother, Pearl, is back on the scene, and Rome's girl, Ngiai, says she's ready to get serious. Oh, and a couple of thugs beat Pearl nearly to death and wrecked Nana's crib.

With everything in their lives out of control, Kwame and Rome are at a serious crossroads. Now they'll have to decide who's really got their backs, and what kind of future they're ready to step up to . . .

### *At the Crossroads*

Franklin "Franky" Bourgeois is fifteen, and he's already done more living than most. For one thing, he was blasted out of a normal childhood in New Orleans when Hurricane Katrina hit. Determined to survive, he left town with two older cousins. They were nothing short of thugs, but they were all he had. And as hard as he tried, even for a good kid like Franky, their influence was hard to resist . . .

Now Franky's just a heartbeat away from a life of crime—until he gets an unexpected chance to turn things around. Getting back on track is easier said than done, especially when a group of high school fools set out to keep Franky on the streets. But Franky's always been a survivor. He'll just have to prove it one more time . . .

Turn the page for excerpts from these exciting novels
by Travis Hunter!

# From **TWO THE HARD WAY**

## PROLOGUE
---
## ROMEO

I paced the rooftop of my apartment complex with a .40-caliber Glock pistol in the palm of my hand, sweat pouring off of my closely cropped head. Fear had a stranglehold on me, and my heart threatened to beat its way out of my chest. I struggled to control my breathing as I eased over to the edge of the building and took in the sight of the only place I had ever called home. That's when I realized that life as I knew it was over.

A nervous chuckle escaped my lips. How dare I ever allow myself to dream of a life outside of this box I was placed in since the day I was born? First my brother's dreams were snatched away, then mine. The more I thought about it, the more I realized my life was doomed from the start.

# 1

## ROMEO

"You ever cheated on Ngiai?" my best friend, Amir, asked me as we walked home from school on a wooded path toward our home in the busted-in and burned-out subsidized projects. Atlanta's Village Apartments had been my home for the last ten years of my life, and although it was a pretty rough spot, I liked it.

"Who is that?" I smiled.

"Whatever. You a player but you ain't stupid."

"I don't cheat. I'm a good boy," I said.

"Man," Amir said, shaking his head. "How you function with all those girls up in your face all the time?"

"The same way you function with none in your face. I just keep it moving."

"What? You crazy. I got more than my share of the honeys, player. I just keep my business to myself," Amir said.

"Yeah, that's not all you keep to yourself. But you should embrace your virginity and stop being ashamed of it."

"You crazy. I lost my virginity a long time ago, lil buddy," Amir bragged his lie.

"Yeah, but Fancy and her four sisters don't count," I said, wiggling my fingers in his face.

"Whatever, homie," he said, smacking my hand down. "Like I said, I keep mine's to myself. I'm respectful of the woman I spend my private time with. Don't need to run around here telling you low-self-esteem-having clowns 'bout my business."

"Yeah, okay," I said.

"What the . . . ," Amir said, stopping in his tracks as we noticed the path to our apartments was cut off by a six-foot-high wrought-iron fence.

"I guess we're moving on up, Amir," I said, running my fingers along the black iron. "I always wanted to live in a gated community."

Amir folded his arms. His face wore a disgusted scowl. He was quiet and his breathing was measured. He seemed to be analyzing the situation we had before us. One of the men working on the gate nodded at me and I nodded back.

"Don't be speaking to no Mexicans, Romeo," Amir snapped. He huffed a frustrated breath, then found his stride along the fence line. "Those people are the worst of the worst. The white man tells them to put up a fence locking black folks in and they jump on the job. No standards. Anything for a buck," Amir said. "You don't see what's going on?"

Amir kept me laughing. He was a walking worrywart who believed the government was secretly conspiring to eliminate the black man from the face of the earth. Maybe that was the reason his hair was turning gray at the tender

age of seventeen. He claimed his dad was a political prisoner, but in reality he was just a prisoner who got caught
selling drugs.

"Nah, why don't you tell me what's going on, Reverend
Al Sharpton Jr.?" I said.

"This is nothing more than the government's way of
preparing us for incarceration. My daddy sent me a book,
and he said the only reason they call where we live the
'projects' is because the powers that be are doing a project on how to eliminate our black butts."

"Your daddy's a genius, dude. You are so lucky that he
imparts such deep wisdom on the world," I said sarcastically. "That's why they keep him locked up, man. He's too
smart to unleash on the world."

"Okay, see, you think this is a game. You're one of those
dum-dums who can't call a spade a spade. I can't believe
you can't see what's going on, Romeo. They tryna condition us to being surrounded by fences. And what does a
prison have? A bunch of doggone gates." He looked at me
like I was the dumbest person ever to take a breath.
"That's what's wrong with black people. We don't think."

"So now you got a problem with black people too?"

His eyes almost popped out of his head. "My *biggest*
problem is with black people. We the worst of the worst."

"I thought you just said Mexicans were the worst of the
worst."

"Hell . . . neither one of us are worth a red cent. But I'll
tell you what—black people are the only group of people
on this earth who just don't care how we look on TV.
We're just happy to be on TV. Master want me to play a
pimp and degrade my sisters . . . Okay." He mocked a
wide-eyed minstrel character. "They be like, 'You ain't

even gotta pay me that much—just put me on TV so people can think I'm somebody and I'll beat that ho to death.'"

I laughed as I always did when Amir went off on one of his race tangents.

"Now, I will say one thing about Mexicans," he said. "They will work."

"Black people work too," I defended. "This country was built on the backs of black people."

"Man, that was three hundred years ago. And we ain't done jack since. I guess we're resting."

"What about Barack Obama?"

"Man, whatever. One man out of two million and you want me to jump up and clap."

"Shut up, Amir," I said.

"I'm just saying," Amir said, sticking his middle finger up at a big poster of a fancy-dressed real estate mogul whose face was plastered on the side of a MARTA bus station. "We done lost all of our pride, man. There's nothing sacred in the black community anymore."

"Why do you stick your finger up at that picture every day?" I asked.

"Do you know who that is?"

"Nope," I said.

"Damn, Rome. You gotta get a little more involved in something other than rap videos and SportsCenter. That's the fool who owns all of these apartment complexes around here. Mr. Slumlord himself. He's riding around in Bentleys and we living in the hood. I don't have a problem with him getting paid, but I do have a problem if he's getting paid from keeping us poor."

"Now, in all of your extensive research, how did you find out that keeping us in the hood makes him rich?"

Amir shook his head again. "It's a good thing you can throw a football, because you 'bout one stupid little boy."

"Enlighten me, Dr. Know-It-All."

Amir shook his head. "Lord, I swear my people are going to perish due to stupidity. The government pays big money to people who take on section eight and subsidize housing. Damn Democrats."

"So you are a Republican, Amir?"

"Not really, I'm Amir. The government is full of crap."

"Shut up, Amir."

"That man on that poster is no different than those slave catchers who used to chase down other blacks for the plantation owner."

"You can find a way to compare everything to slavery," I said, growing tired of Amir's Black Panther moment.

"Okay, name one thing that we as black folks can't find a joke about."

I searched my brain but couldn't come up with anything.

"I'm telling you, Rome. You can think about it until your black face turns blue, but you ain't coming up with nothing. We laugh about everything, a hee hee hee. Even slavery. I bet you won't find a Jewish person laughing about the Holocaust."

"How you gonna judge an entire race based on a few clowns?" I said, getting pulled back in again.

My boy Amir was a character, and I loved getting him riled up. All five-foot-two inches of him. He had a caramel-brown complexion and a big gray patch of hair in the middle of his head. He gave me that Boo Boo the Fool look again.

"We allow those clowns to prosper. We celebrate these fools and make 'em spokespeople for the black community. Have you ever seen the Ying Yang Twins? What about Gucci Mane?"

I had to laugh at that one.

"And that's who we have representing us. I rest my case," he said, throwing his hands up in the air.

"You know, Amir, you should've been born in the fifties or sixties so you could really have something to complain about."

"Oh, you think it's all gravy now, Mr. Dumb Football Player? Racism worse now than it was in the sixties, only now they don't wear white sheets—they wear suits. That's because they're the CEOs of the record labels and television stations. That includes the black CEOs too. If they really gave a hoot about helping blacks, then they wouldn't go and find the most ignorantiest people they can find and put them on TV for little kids to look up to. I swear, I wish I could go on a Nat Turner spree and get away with it."

"*Ignorantiest?* That's not even a word. And you got the nerve to call me dumb."

"It's these public schools, man," Amir said, shaking his head. "But you know what I mean."

Our low-level political debate came to a halt when we saw a few of the project natives standing around a fancy car belonging to a neighborhood hustler named Pete "Wicked" Sams.

Wicked had a few of the locals' undivided attention as he told tall tales of his life as an outlaw. He stopped mid-sentence when he saw me.

"Romey Rome," Wicked called, waving his arm for me to come over and join him. "Holla at me."

"What's up, Wicked?" I said, throwing my hand up in the air and not missing a stride. I knew better. Wicked would have me out there with him all day long talking about what he used to do on the football field. The more he told the story, the better a player he became, and I had heard it so much that by now, to hear him tell it, he was better than every player in the NFL.

"Come here, boy," Wicked called out, which was more like a command.

"I'm in a hurry, man," I said, slowing a little.

"You in too much of a hurry that you can't come and holla at your boy?" Wicked said, playing the guilt card.

Amir shot me a look and shook his head.

"Man, let me go and holla at this fool for a minute," I said, finally relenting.

"You go right ahead. I ain't about to sit up here all day listening to some fool who calls himself Wicked," Amir said. "I'm going home to handle some business."

"A'ight, man. I'll see you later," I said.

"Rock on, black man," Amir said, throwing up his peace sign as he hurried to his building.

"Where the militant midget running off to?" Wicked asked me as I walked over to him and gave him a fraternity-brother-like hug.

"Home, I guess," I said, shaking a few more hands.

"So are you sitting on the bench, or you getting in the game?"

"Don't even try me like that," I said. "How's life treating you, Pete?"

"Beating me down, but hey," Wicked said, rubbing his ample stomach. "I'm eating good."

"I see," I said, eyeing the Buddha-like thing hanging on the front of his body. "You look like you're about six months pregnant."

A few of the flunkies laughed but quickly zipped their lips when Wicked jerked his head in their direction.

"What you do last game?" Wicked asked, turning back to me.

"Threw for two hundred and ran for a hundred, but we lost, so it didn't matter."

"Damn, boy, you the high school all world, ain't cha?"

"Nah, just doing me," I said.

"Keep doing what you doing. I be hearing about cha. You got a lil buzz going round. You know I blew my career up hanging out here in these damn streets. I'm telling you, Rome, I used to be a beast." Wicked's eyes widened with excitement.

*Here we go,* I thought to myself.

"Ray Lewis ain't had nothing on me, boy. I used to break bones. Crack! I'm talking about giving coaches straight up sleepless nights tryna figure out how to block me. Had lil quarterbacks like you in straight panics. Rome, I would've broke you up, boy."

"You too slow, Wicked," I said, shaking my head. "You wouldn't stand a chance."

"You crazy. Ask your brother 'bout me, boy. Matter of fact, come by the crib. I got tapes to prove my word ain't a lie."

"Whatever. I don't wanna see any tapes. If you were all that, then why ain't you in the league?"

"See, my problem was I wanted that fast money."

Wicked spread his arms and nodded toward his black 745 BMW. "Ain't doing too bad, but if I could do it all again, I might've paid for this ride with different dollars."

"It's not too late," I said.

"Look at you. Mr. Opportunistic. Always looking on the bright side."

"You mean *optimistic.*"

"That's what I said."

"No, you said *opportunistic.*"

Wicked turned to one of his flunkies. "What did I say?"

"You said it right," said Mark, a tall skinny kid whose only job on earth was to be Wicked's yes-man.

"Whatever," I said. "How are you gonna ask somebody who failed pre-K to answer a question about a word with more than one syllable?"

"Who you talking to?" Mark said, puffing out his little birdlike chest and yanking the chain of his vicious-looking pit bull.

"You," I said, not in the least bit concerned with him or his dog.

"Mark, shut yo mouth, boy. We can't have Romeo out here hurting up his hands on the likes of you," Wicked said, pushing his flunky away.

"I ain't worried about his hands. I'ma let this damn dog go on him."

"I'm petrified," I said. "Oh, my bad. That's three sylla-bles. I meant to say, I'm scared."

"Come on, Rome." Wicked went into his boxer's stance. "I'm tired of you and all *your* mouth."

I still didn't move. Pete was my older brother Kwame's friend, so he looked at me as if I was his little brother. That was the only reason I could get away with talking to him the way I did. Anyone else would be picking up a few teeth right about now.

"Boy, how old is you now?" Wicked asked.

"Seventeen."

"And you what?" Wicked stood in front of me and placed his hand at his head to measure who was the tallest. "Six feet."

"Six-one," I said, standing up. "You know my brother might be coming home in a few days. His parole hearing's tomorrow."

"Aw, man." Wicked swatted away my concern with his chubby hand. "That lil crack charge ain't 'bout nuttin'. Ain't no *might* about it—he coming home. And you tell him I said come holla at me the minute he touches town."

"I can't wait for him to get out of that place. He's been gone too long," I said, thinking about how much I missed the guy who was far more than a big brother to me. He was also the only father figure I'd ever had. Everything I knew, I learned it from Kwame.

"Two years." Wicked frowned up his face. "Man, that ain't jack. I can do that without a snack."

"Two years is a long time."

"For you maybe, but not for my dog. See you . . . Big Nana sheltered you too much. Wouldn't let you cuss, made you do your homework, and had you up in piano lessons like you was gonna be a black Rocketeer or somebody," Wicked said, drawing laughter from his cronies.

"There you go. I'm outta here," I said, reaching out to tap his fist with mine.

"A'ight. Tell Kwame I said come holla at a player when he gets himself settled," Wicked said, touching his heart.

"Okay," I said, walking away and frowning at the ludicrous thought of my brother putting himself back into the same situation that got him arrested in the first place. I wasn't sure what led to his arrest, because everyone kept the details from me, but I was almost one hundred percent sure Wicked had something to do with it.

"Rome." Wicked stood and shuffled his three-hundred-pound frame over to me. "Hold up, boy. You always rushing off somewhere." He placed a roll of money in my palm.

"What's this for?"

"Just a lil something something. Make sure Kwame knows I gave you that. If . . . When he gets home, give him some of it and tell him I said we need to talk."

I nodded and we shared another brotherly hug.

Living in the Village Apartments, aka "The V," gave you an edge, a hardness that was essential if you were going to survive the everyday rigors of life in subsidized housing. But it was also a trap waiting to close its jaws around you at the slightest slipup. I made my way through the breezeways between the buildings and stopped when I saw General Mack, our neighborhood nutcase and shell-shocked war veteran, marching a line of five-year-olds as if they were in basic training.

"Hut two, three, four. Pick ya legs up, soldier. Hey, pay attention, boy. You gonna mess around and get yourself shot," he sang with all seriousness.

"Good Lord. That man is nuttier than a fruitcake," I said, shaking my head at the spectacle before me. The kids seemed to be having fun, so all I could do was laugh before heading upstairs to the apartment I shared with my nana.

# From AT THE CROSSROADS

Franky was fast asleep in his bed when he was startled by the sound of gunshots. The shots were too close for comfort. He heard them all the time in their neighborhood but never this close. He jumped up and ran out of his room to make sure Nigel and Rico were all right. Nigel was sleeping peacefully, spread-eagle and wearing only his boxer shorts. The gunshots didn't even make him stir. Franky backed away from his room and raced across the hallway to Rico's room. He wasn't there, but that wasn't really that unusual. Nine out of ten nights, he would be on the streets somewhere doing something he had no business doing. Franky walked back to his room and sat on the bed.

*Pow! Pow! Pow!*

He heard more shots. His heart began to race, and he felt helpless. He slid off of the bed onto the floor, hoping none of the bullets would find their way into his bedroom.

*Pow! Pow!*

He heard more shots but this time from a different type of gun. Suddenly, someone was outside of his window. As if he were watching a low-budget action film, he saw someone leap through his open bedroom window and land on the floor with a thud. Franky jumped up, ready to fight.

The boy, who was about his age, give or take a year or two, held his hands up to his mouth, signaling for Franky to be quiet.

"Man, what the . . . ," Franky said, startled to the point where he felt as if he were on the verge of a heart attack. "What do you think you are doing?"

"Please, man," the boy said with tears in his eyes. "These dudes out there tryna kill me."

"Kill you?"

"Yes. Please, man. Please. I beg you to let me stay here for a minute," the boy pleaded.

"I don't know anything about that. You gonna have to get out of here," Franky said, standing up and walking over to his bedroom door. "You can go back out of that window or use the door, but you need to leave right now."

"*Please,* man. I'm begging you. I didn't do nothing, man. I'm not a thief or anything like that, man. I work every day," the boy pleaded through his tears. "I don't wanna die, man. My momma . . . ," he said, then dropped his head. "I don't wanna die."

Franky didn't respond. He stood at the door watching the boy.

The boy popped his head up and started patting his pockets. "Here, I'll pay you." Desperation was oozing out of the boy's eyes.

Something told Franky that the boy was okay, yet he was still wary. People played all kinds of games in the hood. This wasn't some nice suburban area where you could give someone the benefit of the doubt. Franky cursed himself for leaving his window up, but the Georgia heat was making the house a sweatbox.

The boy must've read the hesitation in Franky's eyes, because he started pulling wads of money from both pockets.

"Take it. Here, take it. Just let me stay here for a few more minutes. Please," the boy whispered.

Franky heard footsteps and people talking in the backyard. They stopped outside of his window.

*"Where that fool go?"* one of them said.

*"I don't know. He gotta be round here somewhere,"* the other one replied.

*"That fool got some jets on him. He must be related to Houdini or somebody."*

The boy looked at Franky and held up his hands as if praying to the god of Franky.

"Frankyyyy," a voice called from outside.

"Yeah," Franky said, keeping his eye on the boy and walking over to the window. He turned away from the boy and acted as if he had been asleep. "What's up?"

"You hear anything back here?" a man with a baritone voice asked him.

Franky recognized the tone and knew right away who he was talking to: Stick.

Stick was an older guy from the neighborhood and a complete born loser. He was at least thirty-five years old, and all he did all day, every day was run around the same ten-block radius of Atlanta's west end with kids who were young enough to be his children. He still lived with his mother and was always running some kind of scam. If you wanted a hot television, DVDs, or even the latest Blu-ray players or bootleg movies, Stick was the guy to see. He even sold chicken and steaks that had been pilfered from the local supermarkets. If a neighbor wanted to have lobster for dinner, he would ask Stick and miraculously the seafood would be on his table at dinnertime.

"Nah," Franky said, wiping his eyes. All of a sudden, he felt sorry for the guy who was hiding behind him on the floor, holding his breath for fear that his attackers would hear him breathing. "Is that you out here shooting?"

"Yeah, came up on a lil lick, but the fool got away. He must be a track star or somebody, 'cause baby boy was moving. Messed up my night, 'cause I needed that money."

"Yeah, well, I'm sorry I can't help you, Stick," Franky said. "And use some silencers next time. I gotta go to school in the morning."

"School?" Stick said with a frown. "You going lame on me?"

"Yeah," Franky said.

"A'ight, lil homie," Stick said. "Take your lame tail back to bed."

"You see him?" Rico asked as he jogged up to Stick from the opposite side of the house. "Franky, you hear anybody back here?"

"Nope," Franky said, disappointed but not surprised to see that his cousin was involved in this little scheme with the likes of Stick.

"A'ight, let's walk up this way, Stick," Rico said with a big smile on his face as if they were playing a game of hide-

and-seek. "I know that fool can't be too far away, ya heard?"

Franky closed the window and walked back over to his bed. He sat down and sighed.

"Thanks, man," the boy said. "Those dudes are crazy."

"You sho right about that," Franky said.

"May I use your phone? I must've dropped mine when I was running for my life."

"We don't have a phone, whoadie," Franky said, staring at the frightened boy.

The boy grimaced and rubbed his hands over his face as if the harder he rubbed, the quicker he could come up with a solution to his current predicament.

"Here," the boy said, handing Franky the money. "A deal is a deal. You saved my life."

"What are you gonna do? You can't stay here."

"I know," the boy said. "Can you give me a little time to figure something out?"

"Might as well. You're here," Franky said with a shrug of his shoulders. "But one of those dudes . . . ," Franky started, but caught himself. He didn't know this guy, and he didn't want him returning with the police to take Rico away.

The boys sat in silence for a few minutes before Franky spoke. "Where did you get all of this money?"

"I work," the boy said. "I was over here trying to buy a car, but the guy kept giving me the runaround. Now that I think about it, it was a hustle the whole time," the boy said, shaking his head. "No wonder they kept saying bring cash. Cash only. Cash only."

Franky knew exactly the hustle he was referring to. Take a picture of a nice car, something that young people would like—a Dodge Charger, a Chevrolet Impala, or something like that—post it on a Web site that sells cars, and when the person comes to test drive it, the goons pop out. Some hustlers use a girl to distract the buyer and then they take his money.

Franky held the guy's money in his hand. He leaned over so he could see a little better, then counted the bills. He was holding three thousand dollars.

"It's like eleven o'clock at night. Why would you come to buy a car this time of night, in this neighborhood? Do you have a death wish? Or maybe you just wanna be robbed," Franky asked.

"Nah. I just got off work. I jumped straight on the MARTA," the boy said, shaking his head. "Wow. I could be dead right now."

"Yes, you could," Franky said, handing the boy back his money and standing up. "But you are not, so go home."

The boy held his hand up and refused the money.

"Here," Franky said, pushing the money to his chest. "Take your money."

The boy took a deep breath, then reached out for his cash.

"Just be a little more careful next time," Franky said.

"Man, can I give you some of it? You don't know what you did for me."

"Yes, I do," Franky said, walking out of the room and leading the guy to the front door. "But I would want somebody to do the same thing for me. Take care, whoadie."

"Man," the boy said, looking around when Franky opened the front door. "My name is Davante. I'm not going to forget this. I have to give you something. Here," he said, peeling off about half the bills and handing them to Franky.

"I already told you that I'm good, but since you insist that I take your money, then fine," Franky said, thinking about the empty refrigerator, the bare cabinets, and the past-due rent as he took the wad of bills.

"I'ma come back by here and . . . I don't know what I'm going to do, but I wanna let you know I appreciate this," Davante said.

"Don't sweat it, whoadie," Franky said.

Davante reached out his hand, and Franky shook it. "Be careful out there, ya hear?"

"Yeah," Davante said. He stepped out on the porch and looked around one last time before he took off running.

Franky watched him as he ran straight down the sidewalk without looking back.

The entire ordeal was crazy, but what bothered Franky the most was how normal he felt. He turned around, walked back to his room, and sat down on the bed. He counted his loot and smiled. He was six hundred dollars richer. He stashed the money in his sneaker and lay down on the bed. Before five minutes had passed, he was fast asleep.